For more **Humphrey** adventures, look for

# Summer according to Humphrey

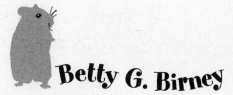

Betty G. Birney

G. P. Putnam's Sons
An Imprint of Penguin Group (USA) Inc.

G. P. PUTNAM'S SONS
A division of Penguin Young Readers Group.
Published by The Penguin Group.
Penguin Group (USA) Inc., 375 Hudson Street, New York, NY 10014, U.S.A.
Penguin Group (Canada), 90 Eglinton Avenue East, Suite 700, Toronto,
Ontario M4P 2Y3, Canada (a division of Pearson Penguin Canada Inc.).
Penguin Books Ltd, 80 Strand, London WC2R 0RL, England.
Penguin Ireland, 25 St. Stephen's Green, Dublin 2, Ireland (a division of Penguin Books Ltd.).
Penguin Group (Australia), 250 Camberwell Road, Camberwell,
Victoria 3124, Australia (a division of Pearson Australia Group Pty Ltd).
Penguin Books India Pvt Ltd, 11 Community Centre, Panchsheel Park,
New Delhi-110 017, India.
Penguin Group (NZ), 67 Apollo Drive, Rosedale, North Shore 0632,
New Zealand (a division of Pearson New Zealand Ltd).
Penguin Books (South Africa) (Pty) Ltd, 24 Sturdee Avenue, Rosebank,
Johannesburg 2196, South Africa.
Penguin Books Ltd, Registered Offices: 80 Strand, London WC2R 0RL, England.

Published simultaneously in Canada. Printed in the United States of America.
Design by Katrina Damkoehler. Text set in Stempel Schneidler.

Library of Congress Cataloging-in-Publication Data
Birney, Betty G. Summer according to Humphrey / Betty G. Birney.   p. cm.
Summary: When summer arrives, Humphrey, the pet hamster of
Longfellow School's Room 26, is surprised and pleased to learn
that he will be going to Camp Happy Hollow.
[1. Camps—Fiction. 2. Hamsters—Fiction.] I. Title.
PZ7.B52285Su 2010 [Fic]—dc22 2009008532
ISBN 978-0-399-24732-3
1  3  5  7  9  10  8  6  4  2

To Desi, with thanks—
"You can learn a lot about yourself
by taking care of another species."

# Contents

# The End (of School)

It was a warm afternoon and there was a lovely ray of sunlight beaming into my cage, as golden as my fur. It made me feel so cozy and dozy, I guess I nodded off during science class. The last thing I remembered Mrs. Brisbane saying was "cumulus clouds." Then I was floating away on my own fluffy little cloud, as peaceful as a hamster can be. *Until* I was awakened by a LOUD-LOUD-LOUD voice that could only belong to my classmate Lower-Your-Voice-A.J.

"How many more days are there?" he boomed.

"Four," Mrs. Brisbane answered.

I opened one eye and listened carefully.

"Just four days until the end of school," she continued.

I opened both eyes, jumped up and let out a loud "eeek!"

"Sounds like Humphrey Dumpty is anxious for school to be out," A.J. said. "Like me!"

*The end of school?* Did she mean that there wouldn't be school EVER-EVER-EVER again? Or was it just another holiday?

"I will miss you," the teacher said. "But it's time to move on."

*Move on? Can a school move?*

"Og?" I squeaked to my neighbor. "Did you hear that?"

Og splashed in his tank a little, then let out a loud "BOING!" That's the twangy way green frogs like him talk.

Stop-Giggling-Gail giggled. "I guess Og is ready for summer, too!"

"Hands, please, class," Mrs. Brisbane reminded her students. She wouldn't be able to remind them much longer. "Yes, Kirk?"

"May I please tell a summer joke?" he asked. At least I-Heard-That-Kirk Chen had learned not to blurt out his jokes without asking.

"Yes, if it's short," Mrs. Brisbane told him.

"What did the pig say on the beach on a hot summer day?" he asked.

"I don't know," the teacher admitted.

"I'm *bakin'*! Get it? Like, I'm *bacon*!" Kirk proudly explained.

"I get it," Mrs. Brisbane said.

Gail giggled again, of course, along with her best friend, Heidi.

There was a shuffle of feet as the clock moved toward the end of the school day.

"Wait-for-the-Bell-Garth," Mrs. Brisbane told Garth

Tugwell. He was always the first one out of his chair.

As soon as he sat down, the bell rang and with plenty of clattering and chattering, my friends in Room 26 hurried out of the room. While they hurried, I worried.

Was it the end of Longfellow School forever?

What would everyone *do*??

And most importantly, where would Og and I go?

What does a classroom pet do when his job is over?

Mrs. Brisbane straightened up her desk, the way she usually did when school was over for the day. She didn't seem bothered about the end of school. In fact, she was humming a happy tune.

I didn't feel like humming.

Maybe Og and I would go live with Mrs. Brisbane and her husband, Bert. I enjoyed staying at their house, but I didn't want to be there all the time without my friends around. How I'd miss Sayeh and Art and Seth and Tabitha and Miranda. Miranda! I could hardly imagine not seeing Golden-Miranda again.

"Eeek!" I squeaked. Again. It just slipped out.

Mrs. Brisbane heard me and walked over to the table by the window where Og and I lived.

"I guess you fellows are wondering what you'll be doing when school is over," she said.

"RIGHT-RIGHT-RIGHT!" I replied, although all that came out was "SQUEAK-SQUEAK-SQUEAK" as usual.

"Well, I can't tell you because it's a surprise," she said.

And then, humming her little tune, Mrs. Brisbane left Room 26 for the day, and left me with a lot to think about.

· ᴖ ·

While my mind raced, I suddenly noticed that it was warm in Room 26. Even a little bit hot. I almost wished I could take off my fur coat. Or that I could swim around in nice cool water like Og. (Not that I ever would, since hamsters should never, I mean *never,* get wet.)

And I'd been noticing for a while that the sky was staying light longer, which makes life a little difficult for a nocturnal creature like me, who looks forward to nighttime.

One reason I look forward to nighttime is because Aldo comes into Room 26 to clean.

"Greetings, friends! You are looking at a happy fellow," he announced as he pushed his cleaning cart into the classroom.

Aldo always seemed like a happy fellow, but that night, he seemed even happier than usual.

"Hi, Aldo! What's new?" I squeaked.

Og added a friendly "BOING!"

"School is out for me! It's over!" He was beaming happily. "And my grades were very good. Even Spanish!"

"Way to go, Aldo!" I squeaked. Aldo cleans at night but goes to school during the day so he can be a teacher someday. He had a little trouble with his Spanish class earlier in the year, so I was happy for him.

I thought for a moment, trying to remember the Spanish word for "good."

"*¡Bueno!*" I added.

"School's out, school's out. Teacher let the mules out," he said with a laugh.

I had no idea there were mules at Aldo's college!

Mrs. Brisbane had been humming earlier in the day and now Aldo whistled as he briskly swept the floors and dusted the furniture. The end of school sure made people musical.

When he was finished, he pulled a chair up close to my cage and Og's tank and took out his dinner.

"No more eating out of paper bags for a while," he said, taking a large bite out of his sandwich.

I liked to watch Aldo eat. His big black mustache made it difficult to see his mouth, so when he ate, the food just seemed to disappear.

"No, my friends," he said. "When Longfellow School closes next week, I'm leaving town! I'm out of here."

I shivered, even though it was hot. There would be no more school *and* no more Aldo?

"Here, buddy, have a carrot," Aldo said, slipping me a crunchy treat as he did every night.

No more treats, either, I thought.

It wasn't just the end of school. It was the end of life as I'd known it.

～·～

"Can you believe it, Sue?" our principal, Mr. Morales, asked the next morning before class began. "Three days until it's all over." Mr. Morales had a collection of special ties, and today, he was wearing a blue one with bright yellow suns on it.

He seemed happy about the end of school, too. But what does a principal do if he doesn't have a school to go to every day?

"The whole family's going to hit the road," he said. "What about you and Bert?"

"We're leaving, too," she said. "Jason's getting married in Tokyo and we're going for the wedding."

Mrs. Brisbane was positively beaming with joy. Jason was her son, and he lived in Tokyo, which is FAR-FAR-FAR away.

So I guess she was going FAR-FAR-FAR away, too. Was that her surprise—*everybody* was leaving?

"What about us?" I squeaked to Og.

He splashed loudly in his tank.

"I guess we'll have to hit the road, too," I said. But it didn't sound like fun.

That night, I dreamed about Og and me on the open road. It was a scary dream because we had to dodge huge cars and trucks that were whizzing by. Once, I saw Principal Morales and his family speed right past us. Then I heard a loud engine buzzing. I looked up and saw Mr. and Mrs. Brisbane waving to us from an airplane. Later, a big bus passed us and a lot of my friends from Room 26 shouted and waved: Golden-Miranda and Repeat-It-Please-Richie and Don't-Complain-Mandy Payne.

Og and I walked and hopped for hours and hours, but we didn't get very far. I was glad to wake up, I can tell you that. And I was tired from all that walking.

But I was happier than ever to see my friends the next morning. I looked around at them. They were smiling, fidgeting, whispering. They looked unsqueakably happy. Why was I the only one who was upset that Longfellow School was closing down?

Nobody seemed to mind the End of School . . . except me and possibly Og.

～•～

The next night, after Aldo's visit, I opened my cage's lock-that-doesn't-lock (it just looks locked, which allows me to get out and have adventures without anyone knowing) and wandered over to Og's tank.

"Whatever happens, Og, let's stick together, okay?" I suggested.

It's always a little hard to tell if Og is listening, because he just stares with those googly eyes and a huge frozen smile on his face.

"BOING-BOING," he said, jumping up and down.

I can't understand everything Og says, but that sounded like he agreed with me.

At least I wouldn't be alone. That was the good news.

But hamsters and frogs have very different likes and needs. That was the bad news.

I decided it was time to take a final walk through the halls of my beloved Longfellow School. Such a fine building—why on earth would humans close it down?

I felt a little sorry for Og as I started my journey. After all, he isn't able to get out of his tank and roam freely, the way I do. Even if he could, he'd probably start to dry out after a while, which wouldn't be comfortable for a frog.

After bidding Og farewell, I slid down the leg of the table and scampered across the floor. I took a deep breath, then slipped through the narrow space under the classroom door.

It was DARK-DARK-DARK in the hallway, though there were some low lights around the school. There was a time when Longfellow School at night seemed mysterious and even scary, but not anymore.

I visited the library first, sliding under the door. Even in the semidarkness, I could see the big aquarium, glowing and alive with brightly colored fish. I scurried forward to take a peek at the little sunken ship lying at the bottom of the tank. It always gave me a thrill—and a chill.

I wondered what would happen to the fish when Longfellow School was no more.

Then I hopped up a series of shelves next to the desk until I reached the top. I pulled hard with all my might and raised myself up onto the desktop. It was a few quick steps to the remote control that was always there. I hit the "on" button and was thrilled to see pictures appear before me on a big screen as music played.

I never knew what I'd see on my trips into the library at night.

This time it was an exciting but frightening movie about a dense jungle with beautiful, dangerous creatures, such as lions, gorillas, tigers and brightly colored parrots. I was gripped by all the howls and growls, the teeth and claws!

When the show was over, I tapped the "off" button, a little reluctantly since I didn't know when—if ever— I'd have the chance to see a movie like that again. I hurried back down the shelves to the floor of the library. Without bothering to glance back at the aquarium and the sunken ship, I scurried out into the hallway, to have one last look around.

I strolled along the darkened hallways, past other classrooms, down to Principal Morales's office. I looked up at the sign that said Principal, the glass window and the suggestion box hanging high up on the big door.

I couldn't reach the suggestion box, but if I could have, I know what my suggestion would have been: Don't close school!

On my way back, I passed the big double doors to the cafeteria. That's where my friends had lunch every single day. I'd always wanted to see it, and this was my last chance. I slid under the door but was disappointed to find that it was a large empty room with tables folded against the wall and not a crumb of food left on the floor!

By the time I got back to Room 26, I was pretty tired, because the hardest part of my adventures comes when I return to my table. I can slide DOWN-DOWN-DOWN my table leg, but I can't slide UP-UP-UP. Instead, I have to grab onto the cord to the blinds, which is very long, then swing it back and forth until I'm up to the table level.

Then I cross my paws, close my eyes and leap onto the table. Whew!

Still, as tired as I was, I had a lot of thinking to do. So I took out the little notebook I keep hidden behind my mirror, and the little pencil that goes with it, and I began to write.

**NOTE TO SELF:** Unlike hamsters, humans love to make big changes. Unfortunately, they almost always forget to tell their pets what's going on.

# The Beginning (of Summer)

The last few days passed quickly.

Mr. Fitch, the librarian, came to Room 26 and collected all the library books. Every last one of them. This was unsqueakably sad to me, because I love the library and I love to hear Mrs. Brisbane read to us. But now, that was over.

Then Mrs. Wright, the physical education teacher with the loud, shiny whistle, came in with a list of games and equipment that my friends had checked out. (I guessed I wouldn't miss *her* too much.)

At the end of the day, Mrs. Brisbane told all of us about her upcoming trip to Tokyo and showed pictures of the wonderful places she would visit—without me.

The next day would be the last day of school. That night, when the door swung open and Aldo said, "Give a cheer, 'cause Aldo's here," I felt happy and sad and all mixed up inside. I was happy because I was always glad to see Aldo. But I was sad, because I didn't know when—or if—I'd *ever* see him again.

"This is it, pals," said Aldo. "Tomorrow, school is over."

"Don't remind me," I squeaked.

"I'll be here tomorrow night," Aldo continued. "I'll be waxing the floors. But you guys will be gone . . . somewhere."

He suddenly stopped twirling his broom. "Where *will* you be?"

My heart skipped a beat. Aldo didn't know where we'd be and I certainly didn't know where we'd be. So who *did* know?

Aldo chuckled and started sweeping again. "I'll bet Mrs. Brisbane has cooked up something special for you. She's one nice lady."

Aldo got through his work early and hurried through his dinner, but he remembered to give me a bit of lettuce. I wasn't very hungry, though, so I hid it at the bottom of my cage. I'd been saving food all week—just in case Mrs. Brisbane *hadn't* cooked up something special for us the way Aldo said.

～⌒～

Way back in September, when a beautiful woman named Ms. Mac brought me from Pet-O-Rama to Room 26, I was excited and amazed to find myself surrounded by so many bright and bouncy students (no frogs yet). Learning about humans was FUN-FUN-FUN, and I also learned to read and write.

The world looked pretty wonderful from my cage until the day Ms. Mac left to go to Brazil and Mrs. Brisbane—who was the real teacher—came back.

It turned out that Ms. Mac was just a substitute.

It turned out that Mrs. Brisbane didn't like me.

It turned out that I didn't like her back!

But over time, I learned that Mrs. Brisbane was a very good teacher who cared about her students.

And over time, she learned that I was a very good hamster who cared about her students as much as she did.

A wonderful thing happened. We came to like each other. In fact, Mrs. Brisbane became one of my favorite humans in the whole, wide world.

Until now. The Mrs. Brisbane I grew to like—even love—wouldn't just head off for a faraway land without making sure I was well taken care of. So maybe I was right not to like her in the very beginning. But that couldn't be! She'd taken good care of me for a long time now.

I was just going to have to trust her and believe that whatever surprise she had in store for Og and me would be something good. Even though I knew from experience that surprises can also be bad things, like meeting up with Clem the dog or Sweetums the cat!

Just in case I was wrong, I stayed up late writing in my notebook that night.

*My last night at school.*

*Things I could do when school is over*
- *Go back to Pet-O-Rama (the pet store I came from—not a good idea)*
- *Teach other hamsters to read and write (Where? Pet-O-Rama? What about Og?)*

13

- *Find a school that doesn't end (How would I find one? In my hamster ball?)*
- *Work at Maycrest Manor (I've already gone there to help people who are sick or injured. Maybe they'd like Og, too.)*
- *Hit the road with Og and roam free (not after seeing those scary creatures in the movie in the library last night!)*

My list didn't look too promising.

❧

The sun came up the next morning, like any ordinary day.

The bell rang and my friends rushed in, like any ordinary day.

But that BAD-BAD-BAD feeling in the pit of my stomach told me that this was not an ordinary day.

"Og?" I squeaked loudly so my neighbor could hear me. "I hope we'll stay together, but if we don't, you've been an unsqueakably nice neighbor and I'll miss you."

"BOING-BOING-BOING!" Og twanged. He splashed so loudly, I thought he'd pop the top right off his tank. He's done that a time or two before.

I felt a little bit better knowing he agreed with me, but I was still worried. I hopped on my wheel for a fast and furious spin, just to let off some steam.

❧

It was a very busy day in Room 26. Mrs. Brisbane collected all of my friends' textbooks but *not* my little notebook. (I keep it well hidden.)

Instead of reading and writing and taking tests, Mrs.

Brisbane and my fellow students were busy packing up their desks and straightening up. Room 26 had never been so neat before!

At the very end of the day, Mrs. Brisbane said that we were the most wonderful students she'd ever had and she knew that we'd all go on to great futures.

That was nice, if only I knew what my future would be!

Then she made a Very Important Announcement.

"Report cards will be mailed out this week," she said. Some students groaned.

"Now, now," Mrs. Brisbane continued. "None of you have anything to worry about."

That seemed to please my friends a lot.

"But there are two students getting their report cards today," she said. "They are very special students who helped make this the best class I ever had."

Then, to my surprise, she picked up two small cards from her desk and walked over to the table where Og and I lived—at least for the moment. She read the first card.

"Og, you have gotten top grades in Water Skills, Loud Noisemaking, Splashing and Being Very Green. All A's," she announced.

My classmates clapped and cheered as she placed the card up against Og's tank.

"BOING-BOING-BOING!" Og twanged.

Then Mrs. Brisbane turned to me.

"Humphrey, you have gotten top grades in Wheel Spinning, Hamster Ball Rolling and Squeaking. All A's."

Mrs. Brisbane hesitated. "But you have gotten an A+ in one other subject: Helping Your Friends. You are truly the most helpful hamster I've ever known."

Oh, how my friends clapped and cheered. They whistled and stomped. Then they stood up and applauded some more.

"Hum-phree! Hum-phree! Hum-phree!" they chanted.

I was just about the proudest hamster in the whole, wide world.

"THANK YOU-THANK YOU-THANK YOU," I squeaked as loudly as I could.

Everything was perfect. Except that little part about *not knowing what I was going to do for the rest of my life!*

"Mrs. Brisbane?" a voice called out.

Someone was speaking out of turn, but for once, it wasn't Raise-Your-Hand-Heidi.

It was Sayeh, the shyest girl in Room 26. Or at least she used to be the shyest girl in class.

"Yes, Sayeh?" Mrs. Brisbane said.

Sayeh stood up next to her desk. "I'd like to thank Humphrey for helping me learn to speak up," she said in a strong voice. "I will never forget him. Not for my whole life."

"You're welcome, Sayeh!" I squeaked.

Suddenly, Sit-Still-Seth Stevenson stood up. "And I'd like to thank Humphrey for helping me settle down. At least a little."

Then one by one, they stood up. Don't-Complain-

Mandy thanked me for helping her meet her hamster, Winky. Pay-Attention-Art said I'd helped him with his math. (And it's not even my best subject!) And Golden-Miranda thanked me for being her best friend.

"And I want to thank Og for being a great frog," Heidi Hopper said. And she even raised her hand before saying it.

Later, Principal Morales came into the classroom. He was wearing a tie that had tiny cars all over it.

"Students in Room 26, I want to congratulate you on a great year," he said. "And I wish you a wonderful summer ahead."

He was in and out of the room quickly, but as he left, I didn't know if I would ever see The Most Important Person at Longfellow School again.

I was happy, I was tired. I was nervous. As the clock went TICK-TICK-TICK, I wondered what my future—and Og's—would be. I hopped on my wheel again and spun.

Then something surprising and wonderful happened. Ms. Mac entered Room 26.

Ms. Mac! With bouncy black curls tumbling around her lovely, happy face. With her big dark eyes and that slight smell of yummy apples. My friends all cheered when they saw her. Like me, they had started off with her as their teacher.

She'd broken my heart when she went to Brazil. But I forgave her when she came back. That's what happens when you love somebody.

"Am I too early?" Ms. Mac asked.

Mrs. Brisbane smiled. "No, your timing is perfect. Please, go ahead."

Ms. Mac was wearing a pink blouse and a bright red skirt and TALL-TALL-TALL red shoes.

"Students," she said, in a way that made the word sound wonderful. "I know you all have exciting plans for the summer. And Mrs. Brisbane has exciting plans, too. But I just want you to know that your friends Humphrey and Og are going to have a fantastic summer, too. Because they are coming with *me*!"

"Eeek!" I actually tumbled off my wheel. Of all the wonderful, fabulous, remarkable and amazing things Og and I could do for the summer, being with Ms. Mac would be the most wonderful, fabulous, remarkable and amazing of all!

"BOING-BOING-BOING-BOING-BOING!" Og obviously agreed with me.

"I'm glad you're pleased," said Ms. Mac. "Because we are going to have a *great* adventure."

I was overjoyed. Og and I didn't have to go to Pet-O-Rama or search for unending schools or hit the open road. We were going to have a great adventure!

I had a big lump in my throat, just thinking of leaving my friends.

But my heart went pitter-patter at the thought of being with Ms. Mac again.

And then, it happened. The bell rang and my friends all raced out of Room 26, out of Longfellow School.

"BYE-BYE-BYE!" I squeaked, but I don't think any-one could hear me.

Og dived into his tank and made a huge splash.

"Well, boys, here comes summer," Ms. Mac told us with a big smile on her face.

Summer! What a wonderful word. I hoped.

**NOTE TO SELF:** Anytime you think humans don't know what they're doing, they'll usually prove you WRONG-WRONG-WRONG.

# 3

## The Mysterious Journey

After my friends left, Ms. Mac and Mrs. Brisbane stayed and talked. They chatted about Mrs. Brisbane's trip and her son's wedding. They spoke about the nice weather. They discussed what a good class it had been.

They talked about just about everything except the great adventure Og and I were going to have.

I thought they'd never stop talking, but finally Principal Morales came in to say good-bye. Then he helped Ms. Mac carry our supply of Nutri-Nibbles and Mighty Mealworms and Og's unsqueakably yucky crickets out to her car.

While they were gone, Mrs. Brisbane stopped and looked at Og, then me.

"It's been a pleasure having you in Room 26, fellows, but I hate good-byes," she said. "So I'll just say good luck."

"Good-bye and thanks for everything!" I clung to the side of my cage as Mr. Morales and Ms. Mac returned and carried Og and me out the door, down the hallway of Longfellow School and outside to the car.

SLAM! The door was shut. Ms. Mac tooted her horn and waved good-bye to Principal Morales and off she drove.

I glanced back at Longfellow School. Would I ever see it again? Would I ever see Mrs. Brisbane or Mr. Morales again?

I was just about to ask Og when Ms. Mac turned up the radio and music began to blare. The windows were open, the music was jazzy and we were on our way—somewhere.

At least I knew that life with Ms. Mac was never ever boring.

~•~

I was a little disappointed over the next two weeks because, although it was nice to be with Ms. Mac again, our lives weren't really that exciting.

Ms. Mac liked to cook and the apartment always smelled of YUMMY-YUMMY-YUMMY things. She had a lot of friends over and they ate the yummy food and listened to loud music and sometimes Ms. Mac played the bongo drums.

To my surprise, Og liked to BOING-BOING along with the bongos!

Still, I have to admit I missed Mrs. Brisbane and my friends in Room 26. Nobody called me "Humphrey Dumpty," the way A.J. did. No one spoke as softly and sweetly to me as Sayeh. And no one giggled like good old Gail!

I was beginning to think my life was going to be an

endless round of bongos and BOING-BOINGs when one day, Ms. Mac got out a large suitcase.

"Og?" I called to my neighbor, whose tank was next to my cage on Ms. Mac's coffee table. "I think she's leaving again! I hope she's not going back to Brazil!"

Og splashed madly. "BOING-BOING!"

I could tell that he had come to love Ms. Mac as much as I did.

"Calm down, guys," Ms. Mac said. "This summer, you're going wherever I'm going. And I think you'll like the place we're going—a lot!"

"Did you hear that, Og?" I was almost crazy with delight. I started my wheel spinning at warp speed. "We're going with her!"

"BOING-BOING-BOING-BOING!" Og twanged.

Even though I had no idea where we were going, I was unsqueakably happy that Og and I were included.

"Of course, we'll have to drive a long way," Ms. Mac continued. "And you'll be in very unfamiliar territory. In fact, it will be just a little bit *wild*."

As soon as she said "wild," I stopped spinning, which is never a good idea because I tumbled off the wheel and landed in a soft pile of bedding, a little closer to my poo corner than I like.

I thought about what I'd seen in the library just a few weeks earlier. Fierce animals with sharp teeth and sharp claws. They were marvelous beasts, but somehow I knew they wouldn't be friendly to small furry creatures like me. Or small green, furless creatures like Og.

Especially at dinnertime, if you get my drift.

Ms. Mac didn't seem worried, though. She was too busy washing clothes and sewing little labels into them.

She packed her clothes and got more food and supplies for Og and me. "We won't be near a town," she explained. "I'll bet you guys will like getting out in nature as much as I will."

"Wait!" I squeaked. "Exactly what do you mean by 'getting out in nature'?" I asked. Because about the only time I'd been out in nature (in A.J.'s backyard), I was inside my hamster ball. And even so, something BAD-BAD-BAD almost happened to me.

"The call of the wild must be answered." Ms. Mac laughed. Then she closed her suitcase and zipped it. "We leave first thing in the morning."

I had to spin on my wheel for a long time that night, trying to get the thought of lions and tigers out of my head. And I tried to tell myself that Ms. Mac was a wonderful human who loved me.

I could trust her. Couldn't I?

～・～・～

When Ms. Mac said first thing, she meant it. The sun was barely up when Og and I were in the car, cage and tank nestled among boxes and bags and pillows and bongo drums.

BUMP-BUMP-BUMP went the little car as it chugged down the road.

THUMP-THUMP-THUMP went my heart (and tummy) with every bump we hit.

23

We drove and drove and drove some more. I couldn't see out the window, so I didn't know if there were any gorillas or lions around. I believe lions can make a lot of noise, but even if they were roaring right next to the car, I couldn't have heard them because Ms. Mac had loud music playing.

After several hours, the tummy-thumping BUMP-BUMP-BUMPs became slower BUMPETY-BUMP-BUMPs and I knew that we had turned off the main road.

Ms. Mac turned off her music. "Ah, there's the sign," she said. "We're almost there."

I crossed my paws and hoped that was good news.

⚬⌣⚬

When you're a small creature who can't see out of the car windows, you learn to listen for clues. Here's what I heard as the car slowed down:

- A crunching sound beneath the wheels, which meant we weren't on a paved road anymore
- More and more bumps
- Birds chirping
- Buzzy sounds

Here's what I didn't hear:

- Other cars whizzing by
- City noises
- People

Then I heard Ms. Mac say, "Oh, wow."

The car stopped. She opened the door and told Og and me that she'd be right back.

The windows were open and a nice breeze drifted in. I didn't smell chalk and erasers and markers and paper bag lunches, like I had in Room 26. I smelled grass and trees and things I couldn't even name.

"Can you see anything, Og?" I asked my friend.

No answer. Maybe the car ride had upset his tummy. He looked a little greener than usual.

I tried to concentrate on the sounds of the birds singing and the buzzy things. Then I heard other noises, too.

SKITTER-SKITTER-SKITTER.

SCRITCH-SCRITCH-SCRITCH.

That sounded like small creatures scurrying about. I wondered if there were other hamsters around.

Then I heard footsteps. Not Ms. Mac's footsteps, though. These were CLOMPITY-CLOMPITY-CLOMP footsteps. Ms. Mac would never clompity-clomp.

Suddenly, a man's big red face with bright red hair under a red and white baseball cap popped right in through the open door!

"Well, who do we have here?" Goodness, his voice was almost as loud as Lower-Your-Voice-A.J.'s.

"I'm Humphrey!" I squeaked back. "Who are you?"

"Yoo-hoo!" Ms. Mac was calling in the distance.

The man's face disappeared. "Hello!" his voice boomed out again.

25

"Hi, Mr. Holloway!" I heard Ms. Mac say. "I was just up at the office looking for you. I'm Morgan Mc-Namara."

Oops! I'd almost forgotten that Ms. Mac had a longer name.

"I remember from your interview. Call me Hap," the man replied. "And welcome to Happy Hollow."

"Did you hear that, Og? We're in a place called Happy Hollow!" I squeaked to my friend. "That's a nice name. It must be a nice place."

"BOING!" Og replied.

Then I heard Hap Holloway say, "I see you brought your friends along."

"Yes, the hamster and the frog, as we discussed," Ms. Mac answered.

"That's us!" I told Og.

"Great! Why don't you get unpacked and then come on up and we'll get organized. You'll be in Robins' Nest tonight. Just up the hill on the right. It's all clean and aired out."

Ms. Mac hopped back in the car and drove up the hill. I was unsqueakably excited. Were we really sleeping in a birds' nest? Would it be up in a tree? Would the robins actually be there? And would a small furry hamster be welcome?

Room 26 suddenly seemed FAR-FAR-FAR away.

**NOTE TO SELF:** No matter what you think humans have planned, they'll always surprise you (like it or not).

26

# Camp Happy Hollow

I wasn't too disappointed to discover that Robins' Nest was not a nest at all. It was a little wooden house surrounded by trees and grass and more trees and more grass.

"Here's our cabin," Ms. Mac said as she gently lifted my cage out of the car.

"Looks nice!" I said.

My, the air smelled fresh, and I smelled something I'd never smelled before. It was the scent of something *wild*.

Outside, the cabin looked like a normal house with a covered porch. Inside, it was a room with four beds—actually, eight beds stacked on top of each other in pairs. Ms. Mac called them bunk beds.

Everything was made of bare wood, except for the red plaid curtains on the windows and the white sheets on the beds. "Enjoy the quiet," Ms. Mac said after she had Og and me settled on a table by the window (she's thoughtful that way) and had given us both fresh water. "It won't last long."

Ms. Mac cleaned up and left us alone.

There we were: one frog, one hamster, one bare wood cabin. No desks, no ringing bells, no shouting children. I missed them all: Kirk's corny jokes, Seth and his sports scores, Aldo's sweeping, Mrs. Brisbane's stories. I was even starting to miss Mrs. Wright. (But *not* her whistle.)

"What do you think of this place?" I asked Og.

Og splashed around in the water but said nothing.

I hopped on my wheel and began to spin. There was really nothing else to do. I tried looking out the window, but it was unsqueakably frustrating. All I could see was green wherever I looked. Green tree branches when I looked up. Green grass when I looked down. Green bushes straight ahead.

Finally, I couldn't stand it any longer. "There must be something else to see," I told Og.

He splashed agreeably. So I jiggled the lock-that-doesn't-lock and the door swung open. I knew it would be difficult (and dangerous) to get down to the floor and outside. So for the first time ever, I climbed up the *outside* of my cage to get a little higher.

I guess I surprised Og with this new behavior, because he let out an alarmingly loud "BOING!"

Standing on top of my cage, I could look above some of the bushes blocking my view and see a teeny-tiny bit more. There were several other cabins in sight—all of them just like the one I was in.

And there were many paths that crisscrossed through the grass.

Mostly, though, there were trees. And more trees.

I was pretty sure there had to be more out there than trees. I knew there were birds, because I could hear them singing. (Thank goodness Ms. Mac left the windows open.)

Then I heard people singing, way off in the distance. I'm pretty sure I heard bongo drums playing, too.

❧

Ms. Mac came in at night, but she went right to bed and got up very early in the morning. She did this a few days in a row. Eight beds. One human. Nothing much to do.

Sometimes I would hear SKITTER-SKITTER-SKITTER and SCRITCH-SCRITCH-SCRITCH.

"Who's making that noise?" I asked Og one day when my curiosity got the best of me. "Is it inside or outside?"

"BOING-BOING!" said Og, leaping around his tank.

"I should probably check it out," I said, but I was almost wishing Og would talk me out of it.

Skittering or scritching could be made by a number of different creatures and some of them might not be too friendly. Still, I am a very curious hamster. Perhaps just a peek would ease my mind.

With a lump in my throat, I jiggled the lock-that-doesn't-lock. I was about to swing the door open when I heard footsteps approaching. I pulled the door back just as Ms. Mac came into the cabin. She was wearing shorts and a shirt that had the words Camp Happy Hollow printed on the front.

29

"You must think I abandoned you," she said.

The thought had crossed my mind, especially when I heard that skittering sound, but I was too polite to mention it. But I was glad to have a reason to stay in my cage.

"I've been in training," she said. "Things are about to start popping."

My mind raced, thinking about what kinds of things popped. Popcorn did and sometimes balloons, which are a little scary for a small furry creature.

Ms. Mac lifted my cage ever so gently.

"I need to get you guys up to the hall to meet the rest of the crew," she said. "I think you already know a couple of them."

I was relieved to get out of the quiet cabin. Ms. Mac carried first me, then Og down a winding path. We passed other cabins like the Robins' Nest, then entered a much bigger wooden building with an even bigger porch and a big sign that said HAPPY HOLLOW HALL.

Inside was an unsqueakably big dining room with long tables and benches. There was even a stage up front with heavy curtains on either side of it. We went through the dining hall, past the kitchen and into a large room behind it.

Ms. Mac put Og and me on a table in front of huge windows that looked out on even more trees and grass.

"Sorry you've been cooped up in that lonely cabin." Sometimes Ms. Mac seemed to read my mind. "You'll like it better here in the rec room. And you'll be busy from now on."

"Doing what?" I squeaked. But she had moved to the door, where she was talking to someone.

"Busy doing *what,* Og?" I asked my neighbor. He wasn't paying attention. He was enjoying the waves in his tank created by our move. They made me feel a little seasick.

I looked around the wreck room. It didn't look like a wreck at all. There were couches and tables and chairs and a fireplace and bookshelves and cabinets—oh, it was a cozy place.

"Meet our first campers," Ms. Mac told whoever was at the door.

I scampered up the tree branch in my cage to see who was coming in. And I almost fell right off again when I saw—well, I couldn't believe my eyes. It was Aldo! He was wearing shorts and a shirt with Camp Happy Hollow written on it just like Ms. Mac.

"Never fear 'cause Aldo's here," he said as he rushed over to see Og and me.

"Aldo! What are you doing here?" I squeaked in disbelief.

"I told you I was leaving town," he said. "I didn't tell you I was coming here to be a counselor. And guess who else is here?" He turned and gestured toward the doorway. "Come here, honey!"

Suddenly, Aldo's wife, Maria, was standing in front of me, smiling happily.

"Maria's taking a break from the bakery to cook here for the summer," Aldo said. Maria worked nights in a bakery while Aldo worked nights at Longfellow School. And I'm happy to say, I helped them get together in the first place.

"It will be the best camp food ever," Aldo assured us. "You guys are lucky this recreation room is so close to the kitchen."

Oh, so the "wreck" room was really a "rec" room! A place for games and fun.

"And I'm lucky that Humphrey and Og are close to me," Maria said with a twinkle in her eye. "I have to do something with the extra fruits and veggies." Yum. I do love fruits and veggies. Og, on the other paw, likes ickier things, like crickets.

❧

More people came in. Ms. Mac called them counselors. Some were grown-ups like Aldo. Some were college students, and there were junior counselors, who were high school age. Ms. Mac brought some of them over to meet me. It was hard to tell them apart because they all had on shorts and identical shirts.

One of the college students, a young woman with short blond hair called Katie, rushed over to see me. "Oh, Morgan, he's so cute! He's the cutest thing I've ever seen!"

I liked Katie a lot.

And there was Hap Holloway. He leaned down and put his big red face right next to my cage.

"Glad to have you aboard at my camp," he said in his loud voice.

*His* camp?

"Just try not to get eaten by a bear," he added, roaring with laughter.

I didn't dare tell him that wasn't one bit funny. After all, it was *his* camp.

It was VERY-VERY-VERY noisy in the room with everyone laughing and talking.

Then suddenly, it got VERY-VERY-VERY quiet. The quiet was broken by footsteps, heading toward my cage.

"Do you think it's a good idea to have *him* here?" a voice boomed.

The way the voice said "him" was very familiar.

I raced to the side of my cage to get a closer look. I knew it. It was Mrs. Wright, the physical education teacher who liked rules more than hamsters. (Let's face it, she *loved* rules and she didn't like hamsters at all. I don't think she was very fond of frogs, either.)

"The kids will love them," Ms. Mac said. I was proud of how brave she was, standing up to Mrs. Wright.

I braced myself, waiting for Mrs. Wright to blow her loud whistle. But she didn't.

"There are health issues. *Allergies.* Disease," she said.

"We're in the woods," Ms. Mac said. "There's lots of stuff to be allergic to."

Then, to my surprise, Hap Holloway stepped forward. "We've got medical histories and releases," he said firmly. "We've got a nurse, too. She arrives tomorrow and she'll sort out any health issues. You can concentrate on being activities director."

Mrs. Wright was speechless, which was a first.

I knew I was going to like Hap Holloway.

"Now it's time for pizza and singing," Hap told the group. "And in the morning, the fun begins!"

Actually, I had a lot of fun that evening. Aldo and Ms. Mac slipped me bits of lettuce and carrots from the salad and I even got a teeny piece of pepper from the pizza.

Katie played the guitar while Ms. Mac pounded the bongos, and all of the other counselors sang amazing songs I'd never heard before. There was a song about a peanut on a railroad track and another one about an alligator. There was something about ears hanging low, which Og probably didn't understand because he doesn't have ears (that I've seen so far).

And my very favorite song was about a bucket with a hole in it. It got sillier and sillier and faster and faster, and silly old me, I was spinning on my wheel and almost fell off, the song was so funny.

If the real fun was beginning tomorrow, I knew that I was going to like Camp Happy Hollow a lot.

Even if I didn't know who would be sleeping in all those beds.

**NOTE TO SELF:** Humans tend to pop up where you least expect them—and some of them have *whistles*.

34

# Happy Campers

After breakfast the next morning (Maria kindly slipped me some yummy strawberries), Og and I watched through the sunny open windows of the rec room as Ms. Mac and the other counselors headed outside and began to set up tables and put up banners reading Welcome to Camp Happy Hollow. Believe me, they were BUSY-BUSY-BUSY.

"The fun's beginning soon," I said to Og, although what I was watching looked more like work than play.

And then a line of cars came up the bumpy road, parking near the hall. The car doors opened and out poured moms and dads and kids of all shapes and sizes. Suitcases, boxes, backpacks and duffel bags came out of car trunks and started piling up near the tables.

"Og, look at all the people! Moms and dads and whole families coming to camp!" I told my neighbor.

Og leaped up. "BOING-BOING-BOING!" he twanged.

Then it came. I should have expected it, knowing Mrs. Wright was around. But the piercing blast from a whistle that is very painful to the small, sensitive ears of a hamster surprised me so much I squeaked, "Eeek!" rather loudly. Not that anyone could hear me, since Mrs. Wright blew the whistle again!

"Line up at the tables and get your packets," Mrs. Wright ordered the families. "Line up, *please!*"

I crossed my paws and hoped the families would line up before she could blow her whistle again. She did it anyway.

"In an orderly fashion, *please,*" she insisted.

Once the families were in line, I noticed something. While many of the faces were new to me, I recognized some of the people in line.

"Look, Og! There's Repeat-It-Please-Richie!" I squeaked. "From Room 26!"

Og splashed wildly. "BOING-BOING! BOING-BOING!"

I climbed higher up in my cage to see what Og was so excited about.

"It's Stop-Giggling-Gail!" I squeaked. There was a flash of blue next to her. "And her brother, Simon." Simon was always on the move.

"BOING-BOING!" Og said before diving to the bottom of his tank.

As I peered out the window at the growing crowd of kids and parents, I saw another familiar face. It was Sayeh. She and her father looked a little bit lost among the bustle of excited families.

"Hi, Sayeh! It's me—Humphrey!" I squeaked at the

36

top of my lungs. Unfortunately, my small voice didn't carry above the hubbub of the crowd.

Luckily, her friend, Golden-Miranda, appeared behind her. The girls hugged and Sayeh's dad shook hands with Miranda's dad. There were two other familiar faces with Miranda. I was glad to see Abby, Miranda's stepsister. She didn't go to Longfellow School, but I'd met her at Miranda's house.

I was not glad to see the other familiar face.

My heart skipped a beat when Miranda's dog, Clem, hopped out of the car. After all, Clem is bent on my total destruction! I've always managed to outwit him—*so far.* Luckily, Miranda's dad quickly put him back into the car, much to my relief.

"Richie! Hey, Richie!" That booming voice could only belong to Lower-Your-Voice-A.J., who had arrived with his friend, Garth, and Garth's parents.

"A.J. It's me—Humphrey Dumpty!" I shouted, using A.J.'s favorite name for me. Again, he couldn't hear me above the noise. Neither could his brother, Ty, who was standing next to him.

Mrs. Wright gave her whistle another mighty blast and Aldo helped her get the people to line up at the tables. Then, one by one, the families hurried off on paths going in many directions and disappeared. They headed toward the cabins, and I figured that each cabin would house a different family.

I figured wrong, because to my amazement, after a

while, the parents all returned to their cars and drove away, leaving their children behind at Camp Happy Hollow!

"Og, they can't leave their children here all alone," I told my neighbor.

"BOING-BOING," Og twanged in agreement.

But they had. I thought for a while and realized they actually weren't all alone. Aldo and Ms. Mac were at camp, and Mrs. Wright and the other counselors. They could help the kids.

And so could I. Maybe—just maybe—a camp needed a pet hamster as much as a classroom did.

⌒•⌒•⌒

It was so peaceful and quiet after the ruckus at the tables that I had a nice little nap. But I was rudely awakened by the ding-donging of the loudest bell I have ever heard. It was even louder than Mrs. Wright's whistle.

Og must have heard it (even if I can't see his ears), because he leaped up so high, he almost hit the top that covered his tank.

Suddenly, the paths were filled with kids wearing shorts and T-shirts, all heading straight for Happy Hollow Hall. Some were laughing and joking, and some looked as if they had been crying. My friend Gail *definitely* wasn't giggling anymore.

There were yummy smells coming from Maria's kitchen, so I didn't think anyone would be crying for long.

Once they were in the hall, I couldn't see the campers, but I certainly could hear them. My friends in Room 26 got pretty noisy sometimes, but there were MANY-MANY-MANY more kids at camp and they were all talking at once.

"Goodness, Og," I squeaked over the racket. "If Mrs. Brisbane were here, she'd quiet them down."

Og splashed around agreeably until there was a loud, shrill blast. Things settled down then and for once, I was almost glad Mrs. Wright was there with her whistle.

I couldn't make out everything that was being said, but I heard Hap Holloway welcoming the campers. Then Ms. Mac taught the kids a song about chewing—I am not kidding! Since hamsters are excellent chewers, I enjoyed the words a lot.

*Chew, chew, chew your food,*
*Gently through the meal.*
*The more you chew, the less you eat,*
*The better you will feel.*

Then the hall got noisy again with talking and the clinking and clanking of forks and spoons. I was getting unsqueakably curious about what was happening in the hall, but I didn't think it was a good idea to slip out of my cage while it was still light outside.

After a while, the whistle blew and things quieted down again. Hap Holloway said something about "campfire" and "games." And then he said, "You'll be getting to know your new friends over the next few days, but I want you to meet two more Happy Hollow Campers."

Just as I was wondering who they might be, Aldo came into our room and picked up Og's tank while Ms. Mac picked up my cage.

Things were really buzzing when we came into the room!

"Humphrey Dumpty!" A.J. shouted, and some of my friends cheered.

"Og the frog!" Garth shouted, and other friends cheered.

Mrs. Wright had to blast her whistle several more times until things were quiet again.

I looked around and oh, my! The tables were filled with enthusiastic boys and girls. Even the ones like Gail who'd looked weepy before had perked up quite a bit.

Hap Holloway introduced us and explained that we'd be staying in different cabins every night and that each cabin would have a chance to earn us for the night by keeping their cabins neat and obeying the rules.

The kids clapped and stomped their feet and I did, too.

Then Hap told them that for the first night, while they were at the campfire, the counselors would be checking out the cabins to see how well everyone had unpacked and made their beds.

There were a few groans, which probably meant there were some unmade beds.

But I wasn't groaning. I was squeaking with joy because Og and I weren't going to be stuck in some wreck of a room from now on.

Og and I were REALLY-REALLY-REALLY going to camp!

**NOTE TO SELF:** Nothing can cheer a person or hamster up faster than seeing an old friend.

# Cabin Fever

The dining hall emptied as quickly as it had filled up. Some of my old friends, like A.J. and Miranda, tried to come up to say hi to Og and me, but a few shrill blasts of you-know-who's whistle kept them moving.

I looked around at the empty tables, the overflowing bins of trash, the stacks of dirty trays and dishes that a teenage boy and girl were collecting.

"What next?" I asked Og.

Og was silent. I guess he was a little confused about what had just happened and what was going to happen next. So was I.

I hopped on my wheel for a little spin and I started thinking of that song that went, "Chew, chew, chew your food." That got me thinking about food, so I hopped off the wheel and rummaged around the bedding of my cage to see what I'd stored there. I found a bit of crunchy carrot, which kept me busy for a while.

Once the teens had gotten all the dishes out of the dining hall, it was quiet again. In the far-off distance, I could hear voices singing. I couldn't catch all the words, but "Happy Hollow" kept coming up.

Then things weren't so quiet anymore. I heard the patter of soft footsteps running, which soon became the clamor of loud footsteps coming closer and closer. The door to the dining hall slammed open and A.J. rushed over to my cage.

"We won!" A.J. bellowed. Even though he was slightly out of breath, that guy still had an amazingly loud voice. "You get to stay with the Blue Jays tonight!"

He didn't get a chance to explain, because the door slammed again. Miranda rushed over to Og's cage. "Og, you're going to be a Robin tonight!" she said. "Our cabin was the neatest girls' cabin."

"Well, ours was the neatest boys' cabin," A.J. said. He grabbed my cage and whisked me out of the dining hall.

"See you soon, Og," I squeaked back to my friend. "I hope!"

The Blue Jays' cabin was just like the Robins' Nest, except the curtains were blue plaid. Each bed had a pillow and blanket on it, and at the ends of the beds were large trunks. Clothes were hung on hooks around the room, and it was extremely neat.

There were boys sitting on the beds and trunks. Some of them I recognized, like Richie and Stop-Giggling-Gail's brother, Simon. Others I didn't, but they all jumped up when I came in and gathered around when A.J. set my cage on his trunk.

"Listen up, guys, this is Humphrey. He was our class

43

pet and he's amazing. So we've got to take good care of him. And we've got to keep this place neat," he said. "We want the Blue Jays to rule, right?"

They all agreed.

"I'll go get him some fresh water," said Richie.

"Me too! Me too!" Simon shouted, following Richie outside.

I soon found out the bathrooms, the showers and the water fountain were outside the cabin instead of inside. (I was lucky to have my water and poo corner inside my cage.)

The other guys in the cabin seemed nice and welcoming.

Then a face appeared close to my cage. "Why's it such a big deal to have a hamster in your cabin?" he asked. "I have a dog. A gigantic dog."

"Wow," said Richie, who was putting the fresh water in my cage.

I was thinking that I NEVER-NEVER-NEVER want to go to this kid's house. *Ever.*

"My dog can do tricks," the boy continued.

"Oh, so can Humphrey," A.J. assured him.

"Yeah, I saw him. He stayed at my house," Simon said.

"My dog is really smart," the boy added. "*And* he's got papers."

"He can *read*?" Richie was clearly impressed, but the thought of a dog reading made Simon giggle just like his sister, Gail.

The boy frowned and shook his head. "I mean he's *pedigreed*. He's like dog royalty. He has papers to prove it."

"His *pet has peed*!" A.J. burst out laughing and the other Blue Jays got to hooting and hollering. I chuckled, too, even though I knew the guy had said "pedigreed."

The laughing annoyed the boy with the dog. He flung himself on his bed and sighed. "How did I end up here?" he asked no one in particular.

I was beginning to wonder the same thing. I was even beginning to think this Blue Jay was not a very nice kind of person.

"Blue Jays rule!" I squeaked without even thinking.

"You tell him, Humphrey," A.J. said.

"He's just making meaningless noise," the unpleasant boy said.

A.J. and Richie exchanged looks. "What's your name again?" A.J. asked.

"Brad," the boy answered.

Things got quieter in the cabin. A.J. came over to my cage and whispered, "Show him what you can do, Humphrey."

He didn't have to ask me twice. I climbed up my ladder and leaped onto my tree branch. I landed pretty hard, so I had to hang on tightly as it swayed back and forth, back and forth. Once I had my bearings, I climbed up to the highest branch and reached up to grab the top bars of my cage. Very carefully, paw over paw, I made my way across the top of my cage while the Blue Jays watched. All except Brad, who was reading a magazine.

"Look at him go," A.J. said.

"Are you watching, Brad?" Richie asked.

"Hmm?" Brad pretended to be too busy to notice.

I took a deep breath, dropped down from my ladder and jumped onto my wheel, where I immediately began to spin.

The cabin-mates all clapped and whistled.

"Hold it down, guys," Brad said. "I'm trying to read here."

"Admit it, Brad. He knows a lot of tricks," A.J. told him.

"Lots and lots and lots," said Simon, jumping around my cage.

Brad glanced up from his magazine. *"That's* a *trick?"*

I could almost feel A.J. getting hot over Brad's bad attitude. He strolled over to Brad's bed and said, "You know we're going to have to compete in the Clash of the Cabins. So what's your sport?"

Clash of the Cabins? He had my attention.

"I don't know." Brad looked a little worried. "I guess I'm okay at all of them."

"Good!" A.J. smiled. "We'll need your help." He swiveled around. "How about you, Simon?"

Simon wrinkled his nose while he thought. "I'm the best burper in our class," he said proudly, and then let out an earsplitting but impressive burp.

Everybody giggled, even me. (Though I know it's really not polite to burp, it can be funny.)

"What else?" A.J. asked, still laughing.

Simon thought for a second. "I never did archery or canoeing before. I'm a good swimmer, though. And I can dive."

"Great!" A.J. and Simon exchanged high fives. "And Richie likes volleyball, right?"

"I've got a pretty good serve," Richie agreed.

"Well, then it looks as if Blue Jays rule!" A.J. shouted. He said it again and everybody joined in . . . except Brad.

"My old camp had a high dive. *Really* high," he said. "This place is dinky."

I saw A.J. clench his fists and I have to admit, I felt my paws tightening up.

Luckily, just then the door swung open.

"Never fear 'cause Aldo's here!" a voice called out.

I thought Aldo had probably come in to clean the Blue Jays' cabin, just as he'd cleaned Room 26 every night. But I was wrong.

He wore his Happy Hollow shirt and shorts and carried a clipboard. "Listen up, guys. It's almost time for lights-out. That means no more talking, okay? Before you go wash up, I just want to go over tomorrow's schedule."

I kept spinning while he talked about canoeing and swimming and archery. Then the boys got ready for bed.

Just before Aldo turned off the lights he said, "No more talking until wake-up call tomorrow morning. Sleep well."

He reached for the light switch. "You too, Humphrey."

Then it was dark in the cabin and quiet. Before long I could hear the boys breathing quietly the way humans do when they're asleep.

I was just about to doze off myself when I heard that sound I'd heard before.

SKITTER-SKITTER-SKITTER.

SCRITCH-SCRITCH-SCRITCH.

The same sound I'd heard back in the Robins' Nest. It wasn't a human type of sound. It was a different kind of sound than I'd heard in Room 26 and at all the houses I visited. It was a *wild* sound. And maybe, just maybe, it was following me!

I was awake for a LONG-LONG-LONG time.

**NOTE TO SELF:** Humans who brag are not pleasant to be around (especially one human named Brad).

# Ghosts, Humans and Other Scary Creatures

That was some wake-up call the next morning, let me tell you. Even from inside my little sleeping hut, the music from a loudspeaker outside made my ears tingle and my whiskers twitch.

I was still twitching when Aldo stuck his head in the door and said, "Rise and shine, boys. Breakfast in half an hour."

Slowly, the Blue Jays rose. I didn't see them shine, but they got dressed and when the bell rang, they headed out for breakfast.

And there I was, all alone and wishing Og was still my neighbor. One thing about camp, people were certainly coming and going all the time. I was considering leaving my cage for a little exploration when I heard the bell, followed by the pounding of footsteps like a herd of elephants coming up the path. The door swung open and the Blue Jays raced into the room.

"Humphrey! We had pancakes-sausage-juice-milk-bananas-strawberries," Simon announced in one breath. Then he let out a tremendous burp, which made all the other Blue Jays laugh, except Brad.

"Food was better at my old camp," Brad said, slumping on his bed again.

No one paid much attention to him.

"Up and at 'em, Brad," A.J. said. "We've got to clean the cabin. Maybe we can earn Humphrey for another night."

Brad rolled his eyes. "Big deal."

"It's a big deal if we can collect enough points over the next two weeks to spend a night in Haunted Hollow," Richie told him. "That's the prize for winning the Clash of the Cabins."

Haunted Hollow? It sounded unsqueakably scary. I was wondering why anyone would want to spend the night in a place with ghosts.

"We all collect points, see?" A.J. explained. "It's cabin versus cabin and boys versus girls. You don't want the girls to get a sleepover in Haunted Hollow, do you? And the chance to see the Howler?"

Howler? Did he say *Howler*?

Just as I was trying to picture what on earth the Howler was, all of the Blue Jays except Brad opened their mouths and let out a horrendous howl!

"Owoooo!!!"

My fur stood on end, but the guys just burst out laughing.

"Who cares about some dumb old ghost?" Brad said. "My old camp had a ghost. We saw him every night."

The other Blue Jays just glared at him. So did I.

"My cousin saw the Howler last year," Richie continued. "He said he was scarier than Frankenstein, Dracula and the werewolf all put together."

Just then Aldo popped his head in the door. "Get those beds made, clothes folded, shoes under beds. Come on, Blue Jays—hustle!"

Soon, the cabin looked exceptionally neat again. When the bell rang again, the Blue Jays raced out, leaving me all alone again.

But almost immediately the door burst open again and A.J. raced back in. "I couldn't forget you, Humphrey Dumpty!" he said, and he carried my cage down to Happy Hollow Hall.

A.J. was in a hurry. I grabbed onto the side of my cage and hung on tightly as he told me that he was going horseback riding for the very first time. From my bumpy point of view, I got a glimpse of large round things with bull's-eye targets painted on them. And a whiff of something that just might have been a horse. A.J. dashed through the dining hall, past the kitchen (yum, what was Maria cooking for lunch?) and into the recreation room.

Whew! I wasn't sorry to be back in front of those big sunny windows. And guess who was already waiting there for me? Og, of course.

"Oggy, old boy! How were things in the Robins' Nest?" I asked. I didn't expect much of an answer, but he surprised me by doing a watery somersault. If only he would squeak up! (But I did envy his swimming skills.)

I quickly filled Og in on what I'd learned about

Haunted Hollow and the Howler, though I'm afraid my "owoooo" was a little too squeaky to be scary. I'm sure Og got the idea.

We didn't get a chance to discuss it any more because Ms. Mac came in with her friend Katie.

"I hope you two don't think you're going to sit around and do nothing all day," Ms. Mac told us. "We're putting you to work!"

I was unsqueakably excited as she picked up my cage and Katie picked up Og's tank, even though I didn't know where I was going or what I was doing.

We headed toward a cluster of small buildings at the top of a hill. But unlike the other cabins, the one we went into had big doors that opened all the way so the front of the cabin was completely open. Down the hill, I saw something blue and glistening, like water.

Inside there were tables and chairs and leafy plants and big charts showing leaves and trees and animal tracks and oh, so many interesting things. Ms. Mac and Katie set Og and me down on a table near the front of the room.

"Welcome to the Nature Center," Ms. Mac said. "You're the nature part. As well as your new friends." She gestured to a tank and a crate farther down the table. "Meet Jake."

I saw a tree branch on the bottom of the tank. Just when I was thinking that Jake was a strange name for a tree branch, it moved!

"He's a garter snake. Very harmless," Kate said.

"Eek!" I squeaked without thinking first. Sorry, but I don't think hamsters and snakes should get too close together. And I didn't like the way his tongue darted about, not one bit.

"Don't worry, Humphrey," Katie said. "We'll keep him away from you."

Ms. Mac pointed to the crate, which was really a large box with openings on the side. "And this is Lovey Dovey. She's a mourning dove we found in the woods with a broken wing. She's almost healed now."

Lovey made a low sound in her throat. "Woo-oo-oo-oo." I think she was saying "thank you" for helping her get better.

"Every day, all the campers have horseback riding and swimming," Ms. Mac continued. "Then they get to choose their other activities, including classes here."

So I was back in a real classroom again!

"Bring on the students!" I squeaked. Then I jumped on my wheel and began to spin, HAPPY-HAPPY-HAPPY to be going to work again.

⁓

In some ways, camp was like school. A bell rang several times a day. At school, I learned those bells meant the start of school, recess, lunch period, another recess and the end of the day. At camp, the bell was even busier. It announced breakfast, cabin cleaning, first activity, second activity, lunch, rest hour, third activity, fourth activity, free time, dinner and the evening program. Whew!

Twice a day, groups of campers came in to take care

of the animals (that's us) and learn all kinds of interesting facts about nature. They had a whole class on rodents (that includes me)! A whole class on frogs! Of course, they studied snakes and birds, too, just so Jake and Lovey wouldn't feel left out. I had to hide in my sleeping hut when I heard some of the things snakes eat. Og and I weren't safe at all. Harmless, indeed!

Sometimes the campers went out and took a hike, but they always came back laughing and happy.

There were differences between camp and school, too. For one thing, I didn't see the same kids all day every day. Since the kids got to pick their favorite activities, certain nature-loving kids showed up time and time again. Sayeh showed up every single day and so did Garth. A.J.'s brother, Ty, was a regular, too, and Miranda was usually around (but she was also very interested in drama classes).

Another difference: there were no tests! I thought this was an excellent idea.

Just like the campers, Og and I got a lot of fresh air and lovely outside sounds and smells. Plus Katie and Ms. Mac got everybody—including me—excited about the wonders of nature.

Yes, I loved the Nature Center very much. I would have loved it more without the snake. I guess it wasn't his fault, but he made me very nervous.

But at least during the day, I didn't have time to think about the SKITTER-SKITTER-SKITTER, SCRITCH-SCRITCH-SCRITCH sounds.

And I tried HARD-HARD-HARD not to think about the Howler. But I was always listening for that "owoooooo!!!"

**NOTE TO SELF:** Humans are unsqueakably smart, but they have an odd habit of liking scary things like dogs, cats and Howlers.

## Night Owls

**H**umphrey, we worked our fingers to the bone to win you for the night." That's what Miranda told me as she carried my cage to the Robins' Nest the next night.

Her golden hair glistened in the moonlight, but I couldn't see her bony fingers, because it was dark outside. I was also distracted by someone asking, "Who-who? Who-who?" over and over.

"It's me—Humphrey!" I finally squeaked back.

Then the someone asked, "Who-who?" again.

"We dusted and swept. Lindsey wanted to wash the windows, but we didn't have a bucket," Miranda continued. "We were determined to have you here tonight."

Inside, the Robins' Nest was clean as could be. Stop-Giggling-Gail was there along with Miranda and some girls I didn't know. They all crowded around my cage, squealing with delight.

"He's *so cute!*" said the girl called Lindsey.

The Robins weren't there long, though. Ms. Mac came in and said, "Time for our first campfire, ladies."

The girls seemed very excited, but Miranda had a question. "Shouldn't we take Humphrey?"

Ms. Mac thought for a few seconds. "Maybe not, Miranda. It might be a little hot and scary for him."

Miranda seemed to understand and the girls raced out of the cabin, leaving me to wonder why anyone would go *to* a fire. Weren't fires hot and dangerous things that humans (and hamsters) should avoid?

Yet I knew that Ms. Mac wouldn't let my friends do anything truly dangerous.

I could smell the faint aroma of smoke in the distance. I jiggled my lock-that-doesn't-lock to make sure I'd be able to get out in case of danger. And I remembered when a firefighter came to Room 26 and told us if our clothes (even fur coats) caught on fire, we should "Stop, drop and roll."

But soon, the girls were back, smelling just a little smoky. Whatever the campfire had been about, they'd certainly enjoyed it.

"Poor Humphrey," Miranda said. "I'm sorry you didn't get to go. You need to get out sometimes."

She took out my hamster ball. "Watch this," she told her friends. She carefully placed me inside, gently set the ball on the floor and there I was, free to roll around the cabin. I hadn't been in my hamster ball in a while, so it took time to get used to everything being yellow again (from the yellow plastic). And it took a little longer for me to remember how to spin around corners and change directions. Every turn I took seemed to amuse the girls.

"Oh, if only Heidi could see you!" Gail said at one point. She plopped down on her bunk and pulled out a notebook from under her pillow. "I'm going to write her about everything you did."

Heidi was Gail's best friend in Room 26. The teacher always called her Raise-Your-Hand-Heidi Hopper, and by the end of the year she did remember to raise her hand most of the time. She wasn't here at camp, but I noticed that Gail certainly brought up her name a lot.

A little later, while the other Robins followed me around, I glanced up and saw Gail staring down at her notebook with tears in her eyes. Was she sad because Heidi wasn't here at camp? I managed to roll the ball right up to her bunk, hoping to get her mind off of home.

"Oh, Humphrey! You're so funny!" Gail reached down to pick up the ball. "When I finish writing Heidi, I'll write my mom and dad to tell them you're here."

Okay. So my idea didn't work.

Later, after Ms. Mac checked in to make sure the lights were out, it was finally quiet in the Robins' Nest. But it wasn't dark for long. There was an eerie light coming from Gail's bottom bunk.

"Hey, what're you doing down there?" Miranda asked in a sleepy voice.

"Just finishing my letter home," Gail answered.

I could see that the light was coming from a teeny-tiny flashlight.

"Lights-out," Miranda said in a very firm voice. "We can't afford to get into trouble. We want to spend the night in Haunted Hollow."

"Okay," Gail answered. I thought I heard a little sniffling, but the light went out.

After the sniffling stopped, it was quiet again and I relaxed in my sleeping hut. A little later, I heard an even more disturbing sound. Again.

"Who-who? Who-who?"

It was coming from outside the cabin, and the voice was strange and mysterious.

"Who-who? Who-who?"

I was tempted to say, "Me-me! Me-me!" but I managed to keep quiet.

I heard one of the girls roll over on her bed.

"Who-who? Who-who?" the voice called again.

The girl got up and went to the open window. "For Pete's sake, be quiet, you old hootie owl!" She clapped loudly and it was quiet again.

"Thanks, Kayla," Miranda said.

"No problem," Kayla answered.

Even though I didn't hear "who-who?" again, I heard other words rolling around in my brain.

Hootie owl! That morning in the Nature Center, Katie had talked about owls. They were strange creatures of the night who like to prey on very small furry creatures—gulp—like me!

Slithering snakes, skittering, scratching sounds, haunting, howling and now hooting.

The wonders of nature were starting to get on my nerves.

When I lived in Room 26, I spent weeknights in the classroom and each weekend, I went home with a different student. But at Camp Happy Hollow, I slept in a different cabin every night of the week—and so did Og. But the two of us never ended up in the same cabin.

The night after I slept in the Robins' Nest, I ended up staying with the Bobwhites. They had taken to imitating the bird they were named for and liked to get in a group and shout, "Bob-*white!* Bob-*white!*"

My old friend Garth was in this cabin as well as A.J.'s brother, Ty, who was only a year younger. It was funny, but A.J. and Garth were best friends and now Ty and Garth were hanging out together.

Then there was Noah. It was a good name for him because he seemed to Know-a-Lot, at least about nature.

"I wish they let us sleep outside," he said, looking out the window.

"Ouch! Mosquitoes." Garth swatted an imaginary insect. "I'll take the cabin."

"I'll bet there are caves out there," Noah said. "I'd sure love to see some bats."

"*Vampire* bats?" Garth asked in a shaky voice.

"Oooh," the other boys said.

I shivered. I'd learned a little bit about bats in school and I'd seen a vampire movie at Kirk's house once. So I knew that a vampire bat was something I NEVER-EVER-EVER wanted to see.

"Not around here," Noah explained. "Just regular

bats. They won't hurt you. They're good for the environment."

"The only bat I want to see is a baseball bat," a boy named Sam said.

"Me too!" I squeaked.

"I want to see the Howler," Ty added. Of course, all the Bobwhites went, "Owoooo."

Like the Robins and the Blue Jays, the Bobwhites spent a lot of time talking about winning the Clash of the Cabins and spending the night in Haunted Hollow. Unlike the other groups, the Bobwhites were pretty sure they'd win, because of Sam.

Super-Sam was what they called him. As in, "You should see him canoeing—super!" Or, "Did you see him pitch today—wasn't he super?"

Apparently everything Sam did was super and he excelled in horseback riding, swimming, diving, softball, volleyball and tennis.

I was happy for the Bobwhites to have such a super—I mean outstanding—camper in their group. But it got a little tiring after a while.

Especially when Garth said, "Turn out the lights, Sam. Super!"

But the next morning as Garth carried me to the Nature Center, I understood why he was so glad to have Sam around.

"You know I'm not very good at sports and things," he said. "No matter how hard I try, my legs just don't go as fast as the other boys'."

"You're not so bad," I squeaked, even though I knew he wasn't so good, either.

"The only way I have a chance of spending the night in Haunted Hollow is if a guy like Sam is in our group. He's so good at everything, we can't lose a game." He continued, "And I *really* want to spend the night in Haunted Hollow."

I wanted Garth and all my friends to get to spend the night in that scary-sounding place if that's what they wanted.

I just wasn't sure I wanted to be there with them.

*Who-who* was afraid of meeting up with the Howler? Me-me!

**NOTE TO SELF:** Beware of things that hoot and howl–especially at night!

## Knots to You

~·~·~·~·~·~·~·~·~·~·~·~·~·~·~·~·~·~·~·~·~·~·~·

**H**umphrey . . ." Sayeh's soft, sweet voice woke me from a short afternoon doze as I waited in the Nature Center for the next group to come in.

I dashed out of my sleeping hut and hurried to the side of my cage where she was peering in at me.

"Sayeh!" I squeaked. "Glad to see you!"

Sayeh smiled, but it was a sad smile. "I wish you could talk to me."

"What's wrong?" I asked. Because I could tell from her face that she needed a friend.

"You know how to get along with people so well," she said. "I'm never sure what to say."

"Just speak up, Sayeh," I advised her. But I know all she heard was "SQUEAK-SQUEAK-SQUEAK," which is one of the most frustrating things about being a hamster.

Sayeh didn't like to speak up. When I first came to Room 26, Mrs. Brisbane was always telling her, "Speak-Up-Sayeh." And over time, with Mrs. Brisbane's help (and mine), she gained the courage to squeak up in class and became friends with many students, especially Miranda.

But she was still what humans would call *quiet*.

"Tell me, Sayeh," I told her. "What's wrong?"

Sayeh pulled up a chair so she could be close to my cage.

"You probably don't even know about the Clash of the Cabins," she said.

"I do!" I squeaked back.

"I was helping Miranda with her backstroke—that's a swimming stroke. But she's a Robin and I'm a Chickadee. Now the other Chickadees say I shouldn't help her." Sayeh sighed. "We were just having fun like in the Happy Hollow song they taught us."

Then Sayeh began to sing softly in her beautiful, sweet voice.

*Happy Hollow—a place close to my heart.*
*Happy Hollow—we loved it from the start.*
*Where we work hard, play hard and have lots of fun,*
*Where it's one for all and it's all for fun.*
*We'll remember forever these happy magic days.*
*We'll remember forever our sharing, caring ways.*
*And for all the days and weeks and years that follow,*
*We'll remember happy days at Happy Hollow.*

Sayeh's big dark eyes turned on me. "You hear that, Humphrey? 'One for all and all for fun'? Wouldn't it be more fun if we could *all* do things together no matter what cabin we're in?"

"It's only a song," I squeaked weakly, but I knew she was right.

"Well, thanks, Humphrey." Sayeh pushed her chair back and stood up. "It's nice to know *somebody* will listen."

I hopped on my wheel for a good, hard spin. While I was spinning, I talked to Og.

"I *like* to help humans. You know that, Og. But I don't see how one small hamster can make a whole big camp more fun," I said. I was huffing and puffing a bit, partly because I was spinning hard, but partly because I was getting a little worked up.

"BOING-BOING-BOING!" Og splashed wildly in his tank.

"Okay, okay, I'll think of something," I told him.

Suddenly, the next group of campers streamed into the Nature Center, along with Counselor Katie and Ms. Mac.

"Okay, kids. Who's ready to learn some more about the wonders of nature?" Katie asked.

A hand shot up and Ms. Mac called on Noah. He was the boy from the Bobwhites' cabin who liked bats and knew a lot about nature.

"Why are these animals in cages?" he asked, pointing to our table.

Ms. Mac explained that Lovey and Jake had been rescued and that Og and I were pets.

Noah wrinkled his nose. "Garter snakes live outside

and they can get along almost anywhere." My, Noah did know a lot.

"And hamsters are related to mice and rats. He'd probably be happier out in the woods," he said.

"Not necessarily!" I squeaked. As much as Noah knew, he didn't understand everything about hamsters.

"I'm impressed with how much you know about animals," Katie said. "But I'm not sure Humphrey would be safe outside. What do garter snakes eat?"

Noah looked up, thinking. "Bugs, worms, frogs, small rodents . . ." he began.

"Hide!" I yelled to Og as I darted into my sleeping hut.

But Noah wasn't finished. "I think we should let them out."

"No!" a chorus of voices called.

"Not if Jake's going to eat Humphrey and Og!" Ty shouted in a voice almost as loud as his brother A.J.'s.

"Calm down now," Ms. Mac said gently. "We hope to get Lovey back outside this summer, if she's ready. But Humphrey and Og are classroom pets. And Jake is kind of the camp mascot."

"Animals weren't meant to live in cages," Noah argued. "They should roam free."

The thought of roaming free at Camp Happy Hollow made me feel all shivery and quivery. Without a cage, what chance did a classroom hamster have when there were hootie owls and Howlers? And when I thought of

Jake out there, the shivers and quivers turned to shakes and quakes.

"We'll talk more about it when we take our nature hike," Ms. Mac said. "Thanks for all the information, Noah."

Noah seemed satisfied . . . for now.

～･～

That night, I ended up in the Chickadees' Nest. Sayeh carried me there, and on the way she said, "You'll make it more fun, won't you, Humphrey?"

She knew I'd at least try.

I must say, the girls in the Chickadees' cabin were very welcoming. Miranda's stepsister, Abby, was one of them. Once upon a time, I thought Abby was mean and crabby, but it turned out that I was wrong. (Sometimes it's good to be wrong!)

I didn't know any of the other girls except Sayeh, but they seemed quite nice. They all watched me climb my tree branch and "oohed" and "aahed" and said how cute I was—perfectly normal behavior for humans.

I think I made the cabin more fun. But then, as on the other nights, the girls left me alone while they went to the campfire. I was still surprised that Aldo and Ms. Mac and the other counselors would take my friends to a dangerous fire. I will NEVER-NEVER-NEVER understand humans (but I'll never stop trying).

Once they were back (smelling a little smoky), Abby clapped and said, "Listen up, Chickadees."

She sat on a large trunk and the other girls gathered around. "Do you know that a girls' group hasn't gone to camp out at Haunted Hollow for five years?" she asked.

A girl named Val groaned. "No way!"

"No fair—right?" asked Abby. "But this year, *we're* going to win. I'm sure of it."

"But how can you be sure?" Val asked.

"Because," Abby began, leaning in close to the circle of girls gathered around her. "I figured it out last year. And I've worked all year to make sure we win."

Abby had my attention, too. "How? What? Huh?" I squeaked.

"Knots." Abby gave the word great emphasis. "Nobody thinks about knots."

The other Chickadees looked as puzzled as I was.

"There are seven areas where cabins get points: Camp spirit—which means stuff like good sportsmanship, cleanliness, being on time—swimming, canoeing, volleyball, softball, archery and outdoor skills," Abby explained. "We're okay in volleyball but probably can't win against the Bobwhites in swimming or canoeing."

"Not with Sam on their team," Val said.

"Yeah, but softball and volleyball are team sports, so he might not be able to carry the whole team. Then there's archery," Abby continued. "A.J.'s good, too. And his brother, Ty."

The other Chickadees all nodded.

"But we could wipe them out in outdoor skills." Abby spun around so she was face-to-face with Sayeh.

"There's a quiz on all that stuff like animal tracks and habits," she said. "Sayeh, you can ace any test, so my money's on you to win that."

Sayeh looked startled. But after a few seconds she nodded and said, "I will try."

So, there were tests at camp after all!

"Trail reading is part of outdoor skills, too. We've got to work on that. But since this is my third year here, I think I can train a winning team there." Abby sounded very confident.

"And then we come to knots. Like I said, nobody pays much attention to the knot-tying competition, so I've been practicing all year on my knots. I can tie knots blindfolded and behind my back. If I ace the knot tying, we've won outdoor skills," she concluded triumphantly. "We just need to hold our own in the other events. Anybody good at archery?"

Val pointed to a tall girl with long braids. "Marissa got a bull's-eye today."

Abby walked over to Marissa. "Fantastic!" she said. "Then we're counting on you. Any questions?"

I raised my paw. I guess I forgot I wasn't in Room 26. But Marissa asked Abby the question I was thinking. "Can we see you tie some knots?"

Abby reached in her trunk and pulled out a handful of rope pieces of different lengths and widths. "Anybody got a watch with a second hand?" she asked.

Sayeh did.

"Time me, Sayeh," Abby said. "First, a square knot."

I scampered up to the top of my tree branch to get a good look as Abby took two ropes and began tying.

According to Sayeh, it took her four seconds.

The sheepshank was next. It took a second or two longer. The bowline looped around and around. Abby went so fast, I could hardly see how she did it. The sheet bend was a very fancy knot, and the Alpine butterfly was most impressive.

"Go, Abby!" I squeaked in encouragement. It was quite a sight to watch her, and no knot took more than about ten seconds.

The other girls clapped and cheered when Abby finished.

"You are amazing!" Val exclaimed. "Even Sam couldn't top that!"

"Thanks," Abby replied. "But let's keep quiet about this. What goes on in the Chickadees' Nest stays in the Chickadees' Nest. And that means you, Sayeh."

Sayeh looked completely surprised. "Me?"

"Yeah. I don't want you blabbing to Miranda about this," Abby said. "I made sure she never saw me practicing."

Miranda's dad was married to Abby's mom, so Miranda split her time between her dad's house and her mom's apartment.

"I won't blab," said Sayeh, but I must say, she looked miserable.

The door swung open and Katie poked her head in the door.

"Lights-out in ten minutes, ladies," she said. "You too, Humphrey."

After the door closed, Abby made everybody raise a hand and promise to keep their plans a secret.

I raised my paw, too. Amazing Abby just might show Super-Sam a thing or two, which might be good.

But Sayeh looked unhappy, which was definitely bad.

**NOTE TO SELF:** Humans aren't so good at climbing, squeaking or spinning, but they have some VERY-VERY-VERY unusual talents.

# Lovey Dovey

It was raining a little bit the next morning. *Sprinkles,* humans call them. Thankfully, not enough to get me wet on my way to the Nature Center.

"I don't like keeping secrets. Especially not from Miranda," Sayeh said as she carried my cage. I clung tightly to the bars of my cage and watched the trees along the path bob up and down.

"I can understand that," I managed to squeak back, though my throat was as wobbly as my tummy.

"I'd love to tie knots with Miranda. We're always braiding each other's hair. It'd be fun if we all got good at knots, but I don't want to let the other Chickadees down," she continued.

"Eek!" I said as Sayeh turned a corner abruptly. "I mean, of course not."

Sayeh sighed. "I guess I'll concentrate on doing well on that test."

"You can do it!" I said, and I believed it, too.

When we had reached the Nature Center, Sayeh placed me next to an empty spot on the table. The spot where Og's tank usually sat. I'd been all set to tell him about Sayeh's dilemma and he wasn't there! Besides, his tank was usually between my cage and Jake the Snake, and not having him there made me just a little jittery. I hoped Jake had been fed that morning.

Sayeh moved on and found a place to sit. Counselor Katie was already in the room, setting up a small projector.

"I think you'll be interested in what I've got for today, Sayeh," Katie said.

I thought I'd be interested, too, as long as it didn't involve snakes.

A few more campers trickled in. I climbed up to the top of my cage to see if Og was coming. Just as I was feeling quite worried, Brad, from the Blue Jays' cabin, entered, carrying Og's tank.

"HI-HI-HI!" I squeaked as Brad plunked the tank down on the table.

"BOING!" Og replied.

"Dumb frog," Brad muttered.

I was stunned. Og . . . a *dumb frog*? Brad clearly didn't know what he was talking about.

"He doesn't even say *ribbit* like a normal frog," he complained.

I scampered down to the bottom of my cage and looked up at Brad. "Now see here," I squeaked. "That's because he's not an ordinary frog. He's a very special frog with a very special sound!"

I wished he could have heard more than just "SQUEAK-SQUEAK-SQUEAK."

Brad wasn't paying a bit of attention to me. He was checking out the Nature Center.

"Welcome, Brad," Katie greeted him. "You picked a great day to come."

"Is this the whole thing?" he asked. "A frog, a bird, a hamster and a plain old snake? My other camp practically had a whole zoo in theirs," he said. "They had a hawk and . . . a raccoon and a boa constrictor!"

Katie kept smiling.

"We try to keep the animals in the wild as much as possible," she explained. "Of course, Humphrey and Og are pets. Some of the workers found Jake under some boards. And Lovey here was a rescue. You'll learn more about her today. Just take a seat."

Brad sat down next to Gail, who was busily writing a letter. She might as well have been at her desk in Room 26. I guess she would have been happier in Room 26.

When the session began, Katie explained that while she was hiking one day, she found Lovey lying out in the woods. It was obvious that her wing was broken.

Then she dimmed the lights and started showing slides. I must say, seeing the lovely Lovey on the ground with one wing just hanging limply was a sad, sad sight. There were even a few drops of—gulp—blood.

"Look at this, Og!" I rushed to get a better view of the screen.

Katie said that it's not a good idea to get close to a wild bird who might be injured. But in this case, it was obvious that the dove was in trouble. When she approached slowly and the bird didn't fight her, she scooped it up with a net and put it in a box. She'd read that mourning doves panic in a cage with bars, which is a little strange to me, since I think the bars on my cage give me wonderful protection from dogs and cats and other scary things.

The next slide showed Katie examining the broken wing with her friend Dr. Singleton at the local Wildlife Refuge. He was a veterinarian who specializes in birds. It made me think of Dr. Drew, who helped me and helped my hamster friend Winky find a new home with one of my friends from Room 26.

The two of them washed the wing and put medicine on it. Then they VERY-VERY-VERY carefully taped the wing back into its original position.

"Og, isn't Lovey very brave?" I squeaked to my neighbor, who took a long, noisy dive into the water in his tank. I could tell he was as impressed as I was.

They gave Lovey food and water and let her rest.

Katie turned off the projector and turned the lights up again. The rain was heavier now, pounding on the roof of the Nature Center.

"Lovey's wing is just about healed now," she told the campers. "If things go well, before you go home, we'll be able to free her back into the wild. Anyone who'd like to be part of Lovey's release, let me know."

"ME-ME-ME!" I squeaked. But there was so much

talking, no one could hear my hamsterish squeaks. In fact, all the campers gathered around Katie, begging to be part of the release.

I looked over at Lovey in her crate. She didn't look like anything was broken anymore. She looked strong and proud.

"Did you hear that, Lovey?" I squeaked at the top of my lungs.

I know birds can't smile, but the look on Lovey's face was as close as a bird could come to a big, fat grin. I think I was smiling a little bit, too, as the other campers left the Nature Center, chattering away.

Brad stayed seated with his arms folded. How could he not think that would be exciting? Ooh, he made my whiskers twitch!

And Gail was still writing nonstop. She didn't even look up.

Ms. Mac went over to talk to her. "You certainly are taking a lot of notes," she told Gail.

Gail looked up. "Oh, I'm finishing a letter to Heidi. I write her and my parents every day so they know everything that's going on at camp."

Ms. Mac looked kind of serious. Then she said, "Why not put away the pen and paper for a little while? Since it's raining, arts and crafts would be a good choice for your next session—you like that, don't you?"

Gail hesitated before folding up her paper. "Yes," she said.

"Come on," Ms. Mac said. "I'll walk you there."

Is it any wonder I LOVE-LOVE-LOVE Ms. Mac?

Then I saw Brad standing and staring at Lovey. Katie came over to him.

"Would you like to help with her release?" she asked Brad.

The boy shrugged. "It doesn't seem like such a big deal," he said. "At my other camp, we had a ropes course. Now *that* was cool."

Katie gave him a curious look. "It sounds great. But this is something different. We could use your help. What was the name of that other camp you went to?"

"White Pines," Brad said in a husky voice. "It was a lot bigger than this."

"Why did you come here?" Katie asked, which was exactly what I was wondering.

"My folks thought this would be a good change," Brad muttered.

Katie kept on smiling. "Sometimes at a smaller camp you can make more friends. I'll be sure to let you know when we're going to release Lovey," she said.

Brad didn't say anything for a while. He just stared at Lovey.

"Whatever," he said.

**NOTE TO SELF:** Humans can be very kind and caring to birds, hamsters and other small creatures. *Most* humans.

# The Thing Beneath the Floor

Whatever! He said *whatever!*" I screeched to Og when all of the campers and counselors had left the Nature Center and gone to lunch. I had to talk extra loud because of the rain.

"BOING-BOING," Og responded.

"What's so great about a ropes course?" I added, though I wouldn't mind some ropes to climb on in my cage.

Og splashed briskly, agreeing with me, I think.

I hopped on my wheel to calm myself down.

"He's always bragging about that other camp," I complained out loud. "His name should be Bragging Brad. And bragging is *bad.*"

"BOING!" Og twanged, so I knew he was listening. Maybe Lovey was listening, too, because she made a little noise in her throat, "Woo-oo-oo-oo." Jake stuck his tongue out, which is what I wanted to do to Bragging Brad. However, I am a very polite hamster.

I was still trying to cool off when the next group of campers began to gather. They were dripping wet, but they didn't seem to mind.

While Gail and Brad and Sayeh weren't having as much fun as they should have been, most of the other campers were. I don't think I've ever seen Garth so happy before. While the campers from the other cabins worked hard on their camping skills and athletic contests, Garth and his fellow Bobwhites seemed to have no worries at all.

Later that evening, Aldo brought Og and me into the dining hall. It was still raining, but the showers were gentler now and Aldo threw a sweatshirt over my cage to keep me dry.

"The kids are pretty unhappy about the rain," he told us. "They hate to miss the evening campfire. But they're in for a big surprise."

"WHAT-WHAT-WHAT?" I asked, hoping it was the good kind of surprise.

"Welcome to the Happy Hollow Comedy Club," he said, gesturing toward the tables. It looked like the regular dining room to me, without the food. He set my cage and Og's tank on a table near the stage. "I know you like to be in the middle of the action, so enjoy yourself."

It was noisy inside while the campers roamed around, laughing, joking, dancing and talking in unsqueakably loud voices. A.J. stopped to say hello to me. At least his voice was loud enough to hear over the commotion.

"How's it going, Humphrey Dumpty?" he asked.

"FINE!" I squeaked at the top of my lungs.

Suddenly, Garth appeared with A.J.'s brother, Ty, at his side.

79

"Hey, Humphrey!" Garth said, leaning in close to see me.

"I saw you canoeing today," A.J. told Ty. "You're going to have to work a lot harder if you want to beat the Blue Jays."

Ty shrugged but Garth turned to face his best friend from Room 26.

"Whoa," Garth said. "We've *already* beaten the Blue Jays. You just don't know it yet."

A.J. looked puzzled. "You're crazy!"

"Not." Garth smiled mysteriously. "In fact, we can't lose. Can we, Ty?"

Ty grinned. "No way can you beat us."

Just then Super-Sam strolled by.

"Yo, Garth. Yo, Ty. Bobwhites rule!" He high-fived Garth and Ty and moved on.

A.J. shook his head. "Sam's good, but he's not perfect," he said.

"Okay," Garth replied. "Just remember that when you're in your bunk and *we're* sleeping out at Haunted Hollow."

Garth and Ty turned to each other and let out a huge "owoooo," which truthfully set my fur on edge a little.

And then it happened. Without warning, Mrs. Wright gave an earsplitting blast on her whistle. I'd be unsqueakably happy if she'd lose that thing, but I have to admit it worked. Soon the campers were sitting down and were even fairly quiet as everyone's attention was directed to the stage.

"Welcome to the Happy Hollow Comedy Club," Hap announced. "Let the skits begin!"

As I said, I had a good view of the stage, and what I saw was quite unexpected. All of the counselors, from Ms. Mac and Katie to Aldo and even Maria, put on a series of little plays—they called them "skits"—that were extremely silly and VERY-VERY-VERY funny! One was about chasing a bear in the woods and one was about putting up a tent.

I especially remember the point where they all put on rabbit ears and sang "Little Bunny Foo Foo." I'm not sure whether it was the song or the sight of Aldo with his big mustache and floppy bunny ears that made me laugh, but I almost fell off my tree branch!

Og splashed around, which almost always means he's having a good time.

At the end of the show, Mrs. Wright took the stage. I braced myself for the whistle, but instead she led us all in singing that song about finding a peanut, which made me wish I had a yummy peanut hidden in my bedding. But I didn't.

When it was all over, Ms. Mac said that next time, all of *us* (she pointed to us campers in the audience) would put on the show, so we'd better get thinking!

Goodness, I couldn't think of any funny songs or skits, but I was going to try.

❧

I spent that night in the Robins' Nest again. It was pretty quiet, even before lights-out. Gail was busily trying to finish a long letter to Heidi. Miranda and the other girls were sharing a magazine and talking about hairstyles.

"Come on, Gail. Let's try this hairstyle on you," Miranda said in a very encouraging voice.

"In a minute," Gail said, still writing. "I made this friendship bracelet in arts and crafts and I want to send it to Heidi." I saw the other Robins roll their eyes and I didn't blame them.

The rain had finally stopped, and once the lights were out for the night, I had a lot to think about. For one thing, I was trying to figure out what was wrong with Brad. Camp Happy Hollow seemed like a wonderful place to me, but to him, the pool was too small, the dining room was too big and the cabins were too far. He spent so much time thinking about his old camp, I'm not sure he even noticed what was going on at his new camp.

Of course, this was my first time at camp, so I didn't have anything to compare it with.

Then there was Gail. Her friends were getting a little tired of hearing that "I'll bet Heidi would love archery" or "I'm going to show Heidi how to tie a lanyard." She must have had a sore paw from writing letters all the time. If she'd stop writing for a day, she'd see what a fun place camp could be.

I must admit, every time she mentioned Heidi, I had a kind of flip-flop feeling inside because it made me think of all the kids in Room 26 that I missed, as well as Mrs. Brisbane, Mr. Brisbane and Principal Morales! I missed the library, the recess bell and even vocabulary quizzes.

But there were so many new things to see and do at Camp Happy Hollow, I tried to think about them instead. I wished Brad and Gail could, too.

It was clear I wasn't going to get a lot of sleep that night. Besides trying to come up with a plan to help Brad and Gail, there was that noise again.

SKITTER-SKITTER-SKITTER.

SCRITCH-SCRITCH-SCRITCH.

In the past, those scratching noises had been somewhere in the background. But that night, they were much louder, which meant that whoever or whatever was making them was CLOSE-CLOSE-CLOSE.

They sounded like they were coming from directly under my cage!

In a way, I was glad the girls didn't hear them. They were deep in sleep.

At least the sounds were coming from *under* the cabin and not *inside* the cabin. I paced back and forth in my cage until my curiosity got the best of me. I reminded myself that I'd gone on dangerous explorations before. So, taking a deep breath, I carefully opened the lock-that-doesn't-lock, tiptoed out to the edge of the table and looked down. Like most creatures, especially nocturnal ones like me, I can see quite well in the darkness and what I saw were wide gaps in between the wooden floorboards.

SKITTER-SKITTER-SKITTER.

SCRITCH-SCRITCH-SCRITCH.

The sounds continued. Since none of the girls stirred when I got out of the cage, I took the plunge. I slid down the leg of the table to the floor. Then I found the widest possible gap and bent down to see what was under the cabin.

There was dirt down there—nice dry dirt. There was a little beam of light from the outdoor lights that helped me see the skitterer: a small furry creature digging in the dirt. It was a hamster! No, its ears were bigger than mine and its fur was not nearly as golden and fluffy. It wasn't a hamster, but something very hamsterish. Something that reminded me of my days at Pet-O-Rama, where I lived until the day Ms. Mac found me.

It was a mouse! A brown mouse, digging furiously in the dirt.

I was afraid of waking the Robins up, but I managed to venture the tiniest possible "squeak!" to get the mouse's attention.

Its head jerked upward so we were looking eye to eye. It froze for a moment and then answered with an "eeek!"

"Quiet, Humphrey," Kayla mumbled sleepily.

Startled, the mouse skittered away and was quickly out of sight.

I was sorry. It looked like a friendly mouse, and a lot livelier than some of my former neighbors at Pet-O-Rama. They mostly napped in their cages and didn't even bother to skitter or scritch.

I was even sorrier when I was ready to get back to

my cage and I realized that there was no way to get back to the top of the table!

Here, there were no blinds. There was no cord.

I was stuck.

It was like standing in a canyon, looking up at a mountaintop with no way to get there.

I thought and thought and thought some more, but there was nothing around that would help me climb that mountain.

In desperation, I crawled into Miranda's baseball cap, which she'd left on the floor near her bunk.

It was a LONG-LONG-LONG wait until morning. There was nothing to do but WORRY-WORRY-WORRY.

In the past, whenever I was found outside of my cage, some human got in trouble for leaving my door open. That bothered me, because the only creature responsible for my being out of my cage was—well—me.

~•~

The next morning, when the deafening wake-up music blared away, I braced myself.

Somebody was going to be in trouble, and I only wished it would be me.

So no one was more surprised than I was when the girls rolled out of their beds and Lindsey scooped up the hat I was in. "Miranda, you'd better be more careful about leaving things around," she cautioned.

Then she set the cap on the table right next to my cage and hurried off to the bathrooms. (Which for some reason they called "latrines.")

I was stunned when I saw the girls all hurrying outside.

Without another thought, I scampered out of the hat, raced to the door of my cage, flung it open and hurried inside. I quickly pulled the door behind me and that was that. My entire night of paw-biting worry was a complete waste of time because no one even noticed I was out of my cage!

**NOTE TO SELF:** Don't worry so much over things that might NEVER-NEVER-NEVER happen.

## 12

# A Sticker-y Situation

It was a sunny day and, as usual, the Robins dropped me off in the rec room, where I met up with Og. I waited there until Katie and Ms. Mac took us to the Nature Center.

While the campers and counselors ate the yummy breakfast Maria and her assistants prepared (*oh, the smells!*), I told Og about seeing the mouse under the floorboards.

"BOING! BOING-BOING-BOING!" he repeated excitedly.

I guess he hadn't seen a mouse before.

Or had he heard a skittering noise in his cabin, too?

Our conversation was interrupted when Katie and Ms. Mac came into the room, even though breakfast was still loudly going on in the dining hall.

"I know I saw a stack of blank notebooks in here the other day," said Ms. Mac, looking through some boxes on a shelf. "Maybe it was this box."

She set the box on the table right next to my cage and began to check what was inside.

"Oh, these are fun," she said, holding up some papers.

"What are they?" Katie asked.

"Stickers. Fun, cheery thoughts to encourage kids. Here's one with a frog on it." Ms. Mac read it aloud. "'I'd be hoppy to be your friend.'"

"It looks like you!" I squeaked to Og, who cheerily BOING-ed.

"Maybe we can find a use for these," Ms. Mac said.

Katie rummaged through another box. "Here they are. They'll be perfect for our nature notebooks."

Then it came: a shrill blast from the whistle.

Katie and Ms. Mac quickly got up. "Uh-oh! It's Ruth Wright. Better go," Ms. Mac said, putting the stickers down on my table.

"Yes," Katie answered with a giggle. "Because everyone is *wrong* except Ruth *Wright*!"

The two counselors hurried into the dining hall, carrying the notebooks with them.

Mrs. Wright not only had a whistle, she had a first name. Ruth. Maybe she annoyed the humans a little bit, too.

I knew what would come next. Morning announcements from Hap Holloway, followed by the camp song and team cheers from each cabin group.

I could hear all that happening in the background, but I was thinking about something else. *Fun, cheery thoughts to encourage kids.* I knew some kids who needed some encouragement. And now, I had a Plan.

Despite the previous night's bad experience outside of my cage, I pushed on the old lock-that-doesn't-lock, threw open the cage door and grabbed as many stickers as I could hold in my mouth. Then I raced back to my cage and pulled the door behind me. Whew!

However, I had a new problem. Where was I going to hide the stickers? I knew I had just minutes—maybe seconds—until the counselors came back to get me.

Then it dawned on me that I had the perfect place: behind the mirror in my cage, where I keep my little notebook.

I slid the notebook out of its hiding place and stuffed the stickers inside, then pushed the notebook back in place.

At that exact moment, Ms. Mac and Katie returned.

"We'd better put those boxes away before Ruth Wright sees we've done something wrong," Ms. Mac said. She reached for the box and caught a glimpse of me out of the corner of her eye.

I was still pushing on the notebook behind the mirror. Had I been caught in the act?

"Look at Humphrey!" Ms. Mac chuckled. "He's staring at his good-looking self in the mirror!"

Katie laughed, too. Then the two of them returned the boxes to the shelf.

It was the second time that morning that I said "Whew!" (But I said it very softly.)

Katie picked up my cage. "Time to go to work," she

said cheerily. "And don't worry, Humphrey. You look handsome as ever. You too, Og."

(I think she was just being nice about Og.)

*— ·∿· —*

Once I was settled into the Nature Center, I saw Brad sitting there. He had a sour expression on his face—as usual—and no one talked to him. He was definitely hard to like, I thought. Yet I'd never met a kid who deep down didn't *want* to be liked.

I guess it didn't help that Gail was sitting next to him. She was too busy scribbling a letter to notice he was even there. I suddenly wished that my old teacher, Mrs. Brisbane, was around. She'd know how to get Gail's mind off home.

Thinking of Mrs. Brisbane made me feel a little guilty. After all, I'd just stolen a bunch of stickers that most certainly didn't belong to me. I'd hidden the stolen goods in my own cage. And I had no idea how to get them to the person who needed them, even though he was sitting in the same room as I was.

I was a thief *and* a dimwit. But at least I was handsome. (I'm just quoting Ms. Mac and Katie on that.)

While I was thinking about my new life of crime, suddenly all of the campers got up and left the room.

"Where are they going?" I asked Og, even though I knew the answer that was coming.

"BOING-BOING."

Og meant well, but I wished he could be more helpful.

Then I had the good sense to look up at the board and see what Katie had written there:

## NATURE HIKE TODAY

I guess I wasn't such a dimwit after all. I wasn't sure how long this hike would take, so there was no time to waste.

"Og, there's something I have to do, but I don't have time to explain it to you now," I squeaked to my friend. "Wish me luck!"

"BOING-BOING-BOING!" he twanged in a way that sounded more like a warning than a good-luck wish.

But there was no turning back. This time, unlike the night before, I figured out my route before I left my cage. It was actually an easy course to get to my goal: Brad's new nature notebook, which was on the floor next to his chair.

I reached behind my mirror and pulled out my note-book. I didn't have a lot of time to study the stickers, so I grabbed the frog sticker and carefully held it between my teeth.

I jiggled the lock-that-doesn't-lock, slid down the table leg and scurried across the floor, straight to Brad's note-book. I carefully removed the sticker from my mouth—the teeth marks were hardly noticeable—and slipped it under the cover.

That's when I made an interesting discovery. Stuck to

the bottom of the frog sticker was another sticker with a big smiley face. It read, Smile! Somebody Likes You!

There was no time to waste, so I pushed that sticker under the cover of Gail's notebook, which was beneath her chair.

Then I dashed back to the table for the more difficult part of my journey.

At Jake the Snake's end of the table was a basket with a TALL-TALL-TALL stalky plant growing out of it. It took strength to climb up the basket, but the woven straw was easy for my paws to grab onto.

When I got to the top of the basket, it took even more strength to leap onto the plant. I climbed up the stem, just as if I were climbing up the tree branch in my cage. When I was level with the table, I held my breath and took a giant leap. I hadn't even thought about how slippery that tabletop might be, but I immediately slid right into the side of Jake's tank. I bounced off and was slightly stunned . . . until I saw Jake.

I'd never gotten such a close look at a snake before (and hope I never will again). He twisted and thrashed about, sticking his tongue out at me.

"Sorry," I squeaked.

Heart pounding, I scurried past him, back to my cage, where I made sure the door was tightly closed.

I checked it three times.

Og splashed around wildly in his water. It took me a

while to catch my breath so I could explain what my mission had been.

I'd barely gotten my story out when the hikers returned to the Nature Center. They were chattering happily, except for Brad. And Gail.

Katie instructed the campers to open their notebooks and write a list of everything they'd observed on their hike. "Don't worry about the writing—just jot things down as you remember them."

Brad rolled his eyes, but he reached for his notebook and opened it up.

Gail also grabbed her notebook, her pen poised to write. But the pen stayed midair as she saw the smiley face sticker in her notebook.

"Watch carefully, Og!" I squeaked as I watched her every move.

Gail studied the sticker carefully. She even turned it over to see if there was anything written on the back.

Then Brad saw his sticker. He picked it up and read it. He puzzled over it for a few seconds, then he began looking around the room.

"That's it, Og! He's trying to figure out who sent it!" I was unsqueakably happy.

Brad looked all around. Gail looked all around.

At one point, they actually looked at each other, but they were embarrassed and quickly looked away.

Soon, the session was over and the kids left their notebooks with Katie.

Gail put her sticker in her pocket. She wasn't smiling, but she did look interested in knowing who liked her.

Brad put his sticker in his pocket. He was still watching the other campers closely. I was pretty sure he wondered who'd be hoppy to be his friend.

Maybe I was a thief and even a dimwit. But at least I'd helped a couple of humans, or so I hoped.

**NOTE TO SELF:** Usually it's not a good idea to be sneaky. But sometimes, *it is.*

# Goldenrod

~~~~~~~~~~~~~~~~~~~~~~~~~~~~~~~~~~~~~~~~~~~~~~~~~~~

That afternoon, Know-a-Lot Noah showed up in the Nature Center, as he always did. Just before the session started, he stopped by our table. "I'm going to try to get you out of that cage, Humphrey. You too, Og."

"Don't do us any favors!" I squeaked to him. I guess he meant well, but I had owls and other scary creatures on my mind.

"I know, I know." Noah acted as if he understood me, though he clearly had not. "You want to be free! I'll get you out of here."

I got that shivery, quivery feeling again, but Ms. Mac was talking and I tried to forget what Noah said. It wasn't long, though, before he was waving his hand.

"Yes, Noah?" Ms. Mac said.

"If we can't free the animals, couldn't we at least let Humphrey get some fresh air?" he asked.

Ms. Mac looked puzzled. "This classroom is in the open air. The front wall is completely open."

"He could walk around in his hamster ball," he suggested.

Everyone, including Katie and Ms. Mac, seemed to

think this was a good idea and soon, I was lazily spinning my way through the rows of chairs. Ms. Mac switched off the lights so she could show some slides of flowers. As I rolled down the aisle, I passed by Garth's chair just as he was stretching his leg and I bounced off his foot. I then rolled to someone else's chair leg, bounced again and picked up speed. Everyone was watching the slides—except me—as my hamster ball rolled through the open wall of the Nature Center onto a small porch.

I stopped moving my paws and let the ball coast slowly across the porch. It was bright outside and the air was very fresh. The rough boards made my ride a little bumpy, but it was lovely being out of my cage and experiencing freedom, like Noah had said. (As long as I had the sturdy plastic hamster ball to protect me.)

Then I hit an especially big bump, took a sharp turn and bounced down three little steps. BUMPITY-BUMP-BUMP!

The ball picked up speed and whirled and twirled its way down a path, veering off to the side into thick underbrush. THUMPITY-THUMP-THUMP!

I was feeling pretty anxious when the ball came to a sudden stop against the trunk of a tree, hitting with such force that the lid of the ball popped open! If I'd wanted to, I could have hopped out of the ball and disappeared into the wild.

I was pretty sure I didn't want to.

While I was trying to figure out my next move, I heard that sound again.

SKITTER-SKITTER-SKITTER.
SCRITCH-SCRITCH-SCRITCH.

"Hello?" I squeaked.

"Eeek!" a familiar voice squeaked.

"Eeek yourself," I squeaked back. "Can you help me?"

That's when I saw the little brown mouse with big, dark eyes peek out at me from behind a tree trunk.

"Oh, it's you," the mouse said. "What are you doing in that . . . thing?"

"It's not a thing. It's a hamster ball." I was a little annoyed with it for even asking. But then I had an amazing revelation. Unlike Og, or Lovey or Jake (who actually didn't make any sounds at all), I could understand this creature, just as I'd been able to understand Winky, the hamster I'd met a while back. Maybe we *were* related.

"Would you happen to be a hamster?" I asked.

"A *what*?" it replied. "Don't be silly. I'm a mouse! A girl mouse."

"I knew that," I admitted. "I've seen mice before. But they were in cages at Pet-O-Rama."

"Eeek!" she squeaked again, her big eyes blinking. "Cages?"

"Never mind," I said. "Can you help push me back toward the Nature Center? I think I've rolled off course," I explained. "If you could push down the lid of this thing, it would help."

The mouse came a few steps closer, but she was definitely on her guard.

"Who are you?" she asked.

"I'm Humphrey. I'm a hamster. A classroom hamster," I added proudly.

"Oh," she said. "I'm not sure what that is, but you look a lot like a mouse. Why don't you come out of that thing?"

It was an interesting question.

"Don't you want to come out into the wild?" she asked.

Out in the wild—me?

"Well . . ." I stalled for time. "Um, I live in a school, in a classroom."

She was clearly horrified. "With *humans*? *Inside*?"

"What's wrong with humans?" I asked.

She shuddered. "They don't like mice, for one thing. Besides, you're not meant to live inside. You should live outside, like me."

I didn't agree with her, any more than I agreed with Noah.

"By the way, who are you?" I asked, only because she'd asked me the same question earlier.

"I'm Goldenrod," she said in a friendlier voice. "I mean, that's what everybody calls me."

"Nice name," I said, and I meant it. "Isn't it very dangerous to live outside? With owls and bats and Howlers?"

Goldenrod looked puzzled. "Howlers? What are they?"

"Oh," I answered. "They're horrible, terrible things.

They're . . . well, I'm not sure what they are. I've only heard about them. They go, 'Owoooo!'"

Goldenrod's nose twitched as she thought about it. "I've never seen them or heard them. Owls are very scary, of course, but bats are nothing to worry about. Yes, there are dangers out here, but it's better than a life in prison. Isn't it?"

"Prison?" I asked. "Who's in prison?"

"I've seen them carry you around in that prison," she said.

I couldn't help chuckling. "That's my cage! It protects me from dangerous things, like dogs and cats."

"What are they?" Goldenrod asked.

"DANGEROUS-DANGEROUS-DANGEROUS creatures!" I said. "You're lucky you've never met them."

"Goodness, I guess I am," Goldenrod replied. "I've seen foxes, of course, and coyotes. But never dogs and cats."

Foxes and coyotes sounded every bit as dangerous as dogs and cats, but I didn't say so.

"Besides, I can get in and out of my cage whenever I want," I explained. "I have a lock-that-doesn't-lock."

Goldenrod tilted her head to one side. "Lock?"

I could see it wasn't going to be easy to explain the role of a pet to her. "Anyway, it's not a prison. In fact, humans love me."

Goldenrod gasped. "Humans *love*?"

I gasped in return. "Of course! They love each other and they love their pets."

"Wow. I had no idea," Goldenrod said. "I thought they just made noise and tore down trees and set fires."

"No," I told her. "They like to feed animals and play games and burp and sing silly songs about Little Bunny Foo Foo."

Goldenrod's eyes got wide. "Bunny Foo Foo? Does he live around here?"

"No." I chuckled. "Never mind."

Then I changed the subject. "Can you help me, Goldenrod?" I asked. "Could you close this lid and give me a push?"

Luckily the ball had stopped with the lid on the side, right at Goldenrod's level.

"Yes, if that's what you want," she said. "It's been interesting to meet you, Humphrey." She reached up with her front paws and pushed the lid closed.

"Oh, and I'll never forget you, Goldenrod. We have a lot in common, you know," I told her.

"I won't forget you, either, Humphrey," she said. "Let me know if you ever decide to be wild."

And with that, she gave the ball a big push and I rolled back toward the Nature Center. I was impressed with her strength.

"THANKS-THANKS-THANKS!" I squeaked to her.

"Bye, Humphrey!" she squeaked back.

I had to run as hard as I could to roll the ball to the bottom of the steps. As I caught my breath, I heard noise coming from the cabin. There seemed to be quite a commotion going on there.

"Humphrey? *Humphrey!!*" That was Ms. Mac's voice, but I never heard her quite so excited before.

"Maybe he rolled under the desk," Katie said.

"Or outside," another voice suggested.

There were footsteps as Ms. Mac and some of the kids ran out onto the porch.

"I hope he didn't roll out here." Ms. Mac sounded worried.

"Wait a second! I see him!" I recognized Simon's voice.

More footsteps and then Ms. Mac reached down and gently picked up my hamster ball.

"Oh, Humphrey, you had us so worried," she said softly. "I guess you had yourself a little adventure."

"You have no idea," I squeaked weakly.

Noah was out on the porch, too. Ms. Mac turned to him. "Noah, you can see how dangerous it can be for a pet to be out of his cage."

"He was in his hamster ball," he said. "But I bet he wishes he could have just kept going."

"That's not for you to decide," Ms. Mac said firmly.

"Right!" I agreed.

In a few seconds, I was safe and secure in my cage. I was glad to be back. And when I rested up, I'd tell Og what happened.

For the moment, I crawled into my sleeping hut for a nice doze. In the background, Ms. Mac was talking about how everybody—even she—was responsible for what had happened.

When I closed my eyes, all I could see was Golden-rod's face. As I drifted off to sleep, the words "I won't forget you, Humphrey" repeated over and over in my mind.

**NOTE TO SELF:** Even a creature who is a lot like you can have very different opinions!

# Problems, Problems and More Problems

That night, the Chickadees had me back again. The boys were annoyed because the girls had hosted me more than they had. But I had to admit, lately the girls' cabins were just a little neater than the boys'.

While the girls were doing well in winning me for sleepovers, the boys—particularly the Bobwhites—were ahead in everything else. Everywhere I went, I heard kids buzzing about the activities outside of the Nature Center.

"Sam hit a home run, bases loaded—he's awesome!" I heard Garth say that morning.

Later, I heard that Sam broke the camp record for swimming laps. *And* that he'd scored the highest number of points in the volleyball game.

Wow, it was true. Sam really *was* super, which made Garth and the other Bobwhites unsqueakably happy.

Still, the Chickadees were far from giving up. Instead of chatting and relaxing before bed the way most of the campers did, Abby had the girls study their trail skills right there in the cabin.

I have to say, Abby sure wasn't lazy. She'd made a

big chart showing the signs they'd have to read out on the trail. The counselors would mark the trail, and to score points, the campers would have to follow the markings correctly and reach the end. Whichever group made the best time won.

It was actually quite interesting. There were arrows and warning signs and even left and right turn signs, all made out of rocks, sticks and leaves. I secretly thought that I would be good at following a trail like that.

The Chickadees seemed tired from a day of swimming-canoeing-hiking-volleyball, but they tried hard to pay attention. Even so, could anyone beat Super-Sam?

Just before lights-out, I overheard Abby take Sayeh aside.

"Listen," she said. "Listen."

I was sure Sayeh was listening, but Abby wanted to make her point.

"I saw you hanging out with Miranda in arts and crafts. If you spill the beans about any of our plans, you'll be betraying the Chickadees and all the work we've put in. Are you with us?" she asked.

"Of course," Sayeh said. "But that doesn't mean I'm not Miranda's friend."

"Fine," Abby added. "But right now, being a Chickadee comes first."

⌒∿⌒

"Did you hear that, Humphrey?" Sayeh asked me the next morning as she took me back to the rec room. "Abby would probably even be mad at me for talking to you."

"I'm sorry, Sayeh," I answered. "I'd never tell a soul."

Sayeh sighed a huge sigh. "I am *not* a tattler," she said.

"Of course not," I agreed.

"I'd love to be Miranda's canoeing partner. I'd love to practice volleyball with her." Sayeh looked very sad. Which made me feel VERY-VERY-VERY sad indeed.

But I had more than Sayeh on my mind because I'd just seen Brad come into the Nature Center. In the past, Brad looked down at his feet most of the time. But today, he was looking at people. He wasn't exactly smiling, but he acted more like he was part of the group.

Gail came in a little later and luckily took the seat next to his, although she didn't seem to notice he was there.

I was staring at the two of them and didn't even notice Noah standing by Og's tank. Goodness, he startled me.

"Og, I found your true home," he said softly. "You need water—lots of it. And other frogs to be friends with. I'll help you, don't worry."

I couldn't tell if Og was worried, but *I* sure was. Og *had* a friend—me! Did he really need more frogs and water? He did quite a lot of splashing with the water he had. If Og's true home wasn't his lovely tank, what was?

I didn't have time to think about Og anymore because Ms. Mac started the session. I crossed my paws, hoping that this would be the day for a hike.

"Okay, campers, who's up for a nature hike?" she asked.

"ME-ME-ME!" I squeaked. I was sorry right away because if Noah was around, he might think I wanted to go on a hike into the wild. Alone.

No one heard me anyway, because everyone was getting up and heading for the door. Luckily, they left their notebooks on the floor.

"Okay, Og," I told my friend. "A hamster's gotta do what a hamster's gotta do."

I grabbed a couple of stickers from my notebook, jiggled open the lock-that-doesn't-lock and slid down to the floor.

I chose a sticker with the outline of a hand on it. A New Friend Is Close at Hand! it read. That went into Brad's notebook.

A Smile Can Work Magic, said the other sticker. It had a magic wand with a star on it. I tucked that into Gail's notebook.

Luckily, that nice tall plant made it easy for me to get back to my table. Now my goal was getting across that oh-so-slippery table without sliding into Jake's tank.

I'd thought about it ahead of time and so I leaned my weight to my left and sailed across the table, narrowly missing the cage and coming to a smooth stop next to Og.

"I made it!" I squeaked.

"BOING-BOING!" Og replied. He'd obviously been impressed with my moves.

I scurried back to the safety of my cage and took a

nice spin on my wheel. When I'd calmed down a bit, I glanced toward Jake's cage.

I thought about what Noah said and wondered if Jake liked living in a tank. I also wondered if he had a way to get out of his tank, like my lock-that-doesn't-lock.

I didn't like what I was wondering. Luckily, it wasn't long before the campers were back.

Brad and Gail weren't exactly smiling, but I crossed my toes and hoped my effort would pay off.

"Okay, nature lovers," Ms. Mac said. "Write your observations in your notebooks."

Brad grabbed his notebook and quickly saw the sticker there. He stared at it for a while.

When Gail opened her notebook, she saw her sticker right away. After she read it, I saw her sneak a quick glance in Brad's direction.

He must have noticed because he looked back at her. "What?" he asked.

"I didn't say anything," she responded. "I thought you said something."

Brad shook his head. "Nope. I'm just writing in my notebook."

"Oh," Gail said. She started making notes, too, then turned to Brad. "Is *ladybug* one word or two?"

"One word, I think," he said. "You saw them, too?"

Gail nodded. "Red ones and kind of orange ones."

"Did you see that purple bird? What was that called?" Brad asked.

Gail wrinkled her nose. "A purple martin, I think."

"I have a cousin named Martin," Brad said, which sent Gail giggling. It was good to hear her giggling again.

"Is he purple?" she asked.

"Nope. He doesn't have wings, either," Brad replied. "But he is short."

Gail giggled again.

"*Because* he's only three years old," Brad added, and they both laughed.

And so it went. Brad never mentioned his old camp, and Gail had a whole conversation without bringing up Heidi or her parents once.

When the session was over, they were still talking as they walked out.

"Did you see that, Og?" I asked my neighbor.

"BOING-BOING!" Og answered.

Even I was amazed at what we'd just seen. And I still had some stickers left.

～•～

Stickers couldn't solve every problem, though. Certainly not the problem the Robins were having, which I learned that night after they returned to the cabin after campfire.

"Listen up," said Miranda. "All the other cabins have skits planned for the Comedy Club, but we still don't have a clue."

"Yeah," Kayla said. "And it counts for a huge part of our camp spirit score."

The Robins looked very, very gloomy as they slumped

on their bunks. (Although, as sad as they looked, I was happy to see that Gail wasn't writing any letters.)

I knew a little bit about the skit planning. I'd seen the Blue Jays outside practicing a funny little play about looking for bear tracks. The ending was a surprise—I couldn't even tell Og about it.

And the Chickadees talked about sitting on an invisible bench, which would be impossible, I think. But every time they talked about it, they burst into laughter. Abby was sure it would be a winner.

But the Robins still had no skit.

"What about the invisible bench skit?" Lindsey asked. "They did that in Scouts last year."

"Ms. Mac said another group was already doing it," Kayla explained.

"That's what we get for being last," Lindsey said.

Miranda began to pace. "I wish Humphrey could talk. Maybe he'd have some ideas."

"Better than ours," Kayla agreed.

I hopped on my wheel for a spin, which is a hamster's way of pacing. Actually, I didn't have any ideas, because I hadn't seen many skits.

The girls were silent for a LONG-LONG-LONG time. In fact, the only sound in the room was the squeaking of my wheel going round and round.

"Hey, Humphrey, could you hold it down?" Miranda got up off her bed and came over to my cage.

"Maybe he wants to help," Lindsey said.

Kayla jumped up and came over to my cage. "Yeah! We should put Humphrey in our skit."

Me, in a skit? I'd never been on a stage before. And the stage in the hall was very big.

"Eeek!" I squealed, and dashed into my sleeping hut.

Then all the girls gathered around my cage and giggled.

"Come out, Humphrey," Miranda said in her friendly voice. "We need you."

When someone says they need me, it's hard for me to say no. I crawled back out and looked up at the smiling faces of the Robins.

"He's so cute," Lindsey said. "Who could ever be afraid of a little hamster?"

Miranda wrinkled her nose. "No one's afraid of a hamster."

"Oh, yeah," Lindsey replied. "My mom. We had a hamster named Chip and he got out of his cage and my mom started screaming and got up on a *chair*! Like he was a monster or something. My brother and I laughed so hard we cried." Lindsey wasn't crying now. She was laughing and so were her friends.

"That'd be funny," Miranda said. "If someone was afraid of Humphrey."

Then the most amazing thing happened. The girls started chattering and then they started acting things out. Sometimes they agreed and sometimes they disagreed, but they began to work out a skit that looked pretty interesting. Until they got to the last part.

"And that's where Humphrey comes in," Gail said. She was giggling again and I was glad.

"You'll help us, Humphrey? Won't you?" Miranda asked.

I could never say "no" to Golden-Miranda.

❧

By the time Ms. Mac came in for lights-out, we'd rehearsed the skit several times. The Robins begged her to stay so we could act it out for her. She loved it but suggested they needed a few more people.

"Counselor Katie and I would love to help out," she said.

The girls all cheered.

"So where'd you come up with the idea?" Ms. Mac asked.

The Robins all pointed to my cage. "Humphrey!" they said.

Ms. Mac smiled. "Who else?"

❧

Later that night, I looked up at the moon through an open spot in the curtains. It reminded me of a big spotlight. Like a spotlight shining on a stage.

A BIG-BIG-BIG stage for a SMALL-SMALL-SMALL hamster. I spun on my wheel for a long time.

**NOTE TO SELF:** When you offer to give someone a helping paw, you'd better mean it—because you might end up a lot more involved than you ever dreamed.

# A Taste of Freedom

Guys, it's not going to be easy," A.J. announced the next night in the Blue Jays' cabin. They'd worked extra hard to win me for the night. "We're getting massacred by the Bobwhites, all because of that stupid Sam. Why'd he have to come to camp?"

"Yeah," Richie agreed. "Why didn't he go to that camp Brad's always bragging about? The one that's so much better than Happy Hollow?"

I glanced over at Brad, who was sitting on his bunk.

"It wasn't that great," he said.

That got everybody's attention—especially mine!

"This camp isn't so bad," he admitted. "The pool is smaller, but White Pines didn't have a lake. I like canoeing. In fact, I tied Sam today in the race across the lake."

A.J.'s jaw dropped. "You did?"

"I was thinking," Brad continued. "I've been spending a lot of time at the Nature Center and I might do pretty well on the nature quiz. And the canoeing would help our score. And what about that knot-tying thing—I mean doesn't that just take practice?"

"I forgot about that," A.J. admitted. "Has anybody been working on it?"

The other Blue Jays shook their heads.

"I could practice that," Simon volunteered. "I practiced burping for months and look how well that turned out." He let out another thunderous burp, which made everybody laugh.

Simon was always moving . . . but maybe if he put all that energy into one thing—like knot tying—it just might work.

"The Bobwhites are depending on Sam," A.J. said. "But that's no reason for us to give up. Blue Jays rule!"

They all cheered and high-fived—even Brad. At least for that night, I thought that even Super-Sam couldn't defeat the Blue Jays.

By the next afternoon, I was not as convinced. Sam got a bull's-eye in archery and pitched the winning softball game. He was amazing, all right. So where did that leave everybody else?

~·∾·~

That night, I heard the noises under the cabin.

SKITTER-SKITTER-SKITTER.

SCRITCH-SCRITCH-SCRITCH.

"Hi, Goldenrod!" I squeaked softly.

"Hi, Humphrey," she answered. "Won't you join me? Someone dropped some lovely peanuts under the floorboards."

"Thanks a lot, but I had dinner," I said.

She went back to scratching in the dirt. I still wondered what it would be like to live her life.

But I had too many things to worry about to wonder for long.

The next morning, Miranda and Kayla stopped by the rec room after breakfast. Ms. Mac was already there, getting her supplies for the day.

"Ms. Mac?" Miranda said. "Can we ask you something?"

"Anything at all." Ms. Mac's hands were full of markers and glue sticks.

"We were just thinking, maybe Noah is right," Miranda continued nervously. "About Humphrey."

Ms. Mac looked amazed. "You don't think we should set him free?" she asked.

"Eeek!" I had to squeak up before things went too far.

"No," Miranda said. "But he hasn't seen very much of camp. He's just been cooped up in the Nature Center."

It was true. I heard my friends talk about canoeing and swimming and archery, but I hadn't seen any of that. And where were those horses they talked about? I wanted to see more of camp—but from inside my cage.

The girls asked Ms. Mac if they could take me out of the Nature Center that afternoon and give me a tour.

Ms. Mac thought for a while before answering. "You girls are very responsible. Yes, I guess so," she said. "As long as you absolutely *promise* not to let him out of his cage."

The girls promised and soon, Miranda and Kayla had enlisted Sayeh and Abby to help them show me around Camp Happy Hollow.

And oh, what a place it was! So much bigger than what I imagined just traveling from the cabins to the Nature Center to Happy Hollow Hall.

There was the softball diamond, the volleyball court, the archery range. (I was glad no one was around since I wasn't interested in dodging sharp arrows!)

There were horses, too—the biggest creatures I'd ever seen—or hoped to see! Their hooves were gigantic and they must weigh a million pounds! And sitting right on top of one huge beast was A.J.

"Hi, Humphrey Dumpty!" he shouted.

I closed my eyes, hoping his loud voice wouldn't scare the horse. (It didn't.)

We moved on, passing by a deep blue swimming pool. And who was diving off the diving board? Super-Sam, of course.

Then the girls took me out to the lake.

"We've saved the best for last," Miranda said. "Welcome to Lake Lavender."

Though I'd been sailing once before (quite unexpectedly), I'd never seen such a large and thrilling stretch of water. There was a dock with canoes lined up, and just for one teeny-tiny second, I almost wished I could be a human! But then I realized that being a hamster gave me the chance to do and see things humans never could.

And humans seem to have so many problems—I was only glad I'm around to lend a helping paw from time to time.

"What do you think, Humphrey?" Sayeh asked as we gazed out at the rippling water.

"It's breathtaking!" I exclaimed.

And it was. With the blue of the lake and the blue of the sky and the—what was that circling in the blue sky? I squinted to get a better view of a very large bird.

"Oh, look! A hawk!" said Abby.

Oh, no! A hawk! Katie had talked about them, too. They were not friends to small furry creatures.

"Eeek!" I squeaked, and the girls all giggled.

But the lake was lovely. How Og would like it! It was hard to see water without thinking of my friend, whom I was beginning to miss.

Next the girls carried my cage up to the top of a hill. From way up there, I could see the camp nestled into a low spot.

"There it is, Humphrey. That valley there—that's Happy Hollow," Kayla said. So that's where the camp got its name!

Miranda swung my cage around to another hollow right next to the camp. "And that's Haunted Hollow," she said in an ominous tone of voice. "Where one group will get to spend the night."

"Yeah, the Chickadees!" said Abby.

Miranda looked a little surprised. "Or the Robins," she countered.

Abby folded her arms and shook her head. "Sorry, Miranda. We've got it nailed. Right, Sayeh?"

I swiveled around in my cage to see Sayeh's face. She looked surprised and upset at the question.

"May the best team win," Miranda said. Then she added, "And that will be us!"

I wasn't sure who the best team was. And I wasn't at all sure who would win.

~•~

When we got back down to camp, something had changed. There was a group of campers gathered around a tree. And another group gathered around the next tree.

"I wonder what's going on?" Miranda said.

Once we got closer, I could see another clump of kids staring up at the side of the Nature Center.

"Come on," Kayla said, and we picked up our pace (which made it a tummy-wobbling trip).

When we reached the first tree, Miranda elbowed her way through the small crowd.

"What's up?" she said.

"This is up." Richie pointed at a handmade sign tacked to the tree trunk.

### FREE THE AMINALS!
### RELEASE OUR WILD AMINALS!

(Even though it was spelled "Aminals," I think we all knew what it meant.)

In smaller letters underneath, the signs said:

### FREE LOVEY, JAKE, OG, HUMFRY.

117

(The sign maker was definitely not a good speller.)

"Eeek!" I said without even thinking.

"Free Humphrey?" Miranda sounded truly puzzled.

"That's not right," Sayeh added.

"I am not a wild animal!" I protested. "Or aminal!"

"He is not a wild animal," Sayeh repeated, even though she probably didn't understand what I'd said. We just thought alike.

Just then Counselor Katie approached. When she saw all the kids gathered, she came up to check things out. "What's going on?" she asked.

"This." Miranda pointed to the sign.

Katie studied the sign and said, "Oh." She stuffed her hands into the pockets of her shorts and asked, "Who put this up?"

"Duh," Richie said. "It must be Noah. All he talks about is animals."

Now, talking about animals is not a bad thing. In fact, I usually think it's a very good thing.

But even though Noah cared a lot about animals—and he did—I was almost as frightened of him as I was of the hootie owl, the hawk and the Howler.

"I'll talk to him," Katie said.

She left and the campers scattered. Miranda took me back to the Nature Center and set me on the table next to Og.

We were alone then, except for Lovey and Jake, who were on the other end of the table.

I was still thinking about that hawk.

"Listen, Og," I said. "Noah wants to free us. But I've been out there and I just want to say, you might not *want* to be free."

"BOING." It was a quiet response.

"I'm just saying there are some dangerous creatures out there who are our enemies. They don't like hamsters and frogs at all, except maybe for dinner." I realized I was getting slightly hysterical. "Like owls and hawks and snakes!"

I was sorry as soon as I said it. I craned my neck to try and see Jake in his cage, but Lovey's crate blocked him.

"Maybe you don't feel that way, Jake," I said. My voice was a little weak. "I'm sure you're a friendly snake, like I'm a friendly hamster and Og's a friendly frog," I added, hoping it would help.

I'm afraid I didn't sound very convincing.

I crossed my paws and HOPED-HOPED-HOPED that I would not spend the night with the Bobwhites—and Noah—that particular night.

**NOTE TO SELF:** It's great to be free–but only when you want to be!

# Onstage at the Comedy Club

Despite the disturbing signs, my day out had done me a world of good and I was planning on a long, dozy evening in somebody's cabin.

But I had forgotten one thing: it was Happy Hollow Comedy Club night. And as much as I would have liked a nap, I knew I wouldn't get one.

After dinner, Aldo brought Og and me into the dining hall and gave us a ringside seat near the stage. It looked a lot bigger than it ever had before.

I was concentrating on remembering my part when Hap Holloway came out onstage with a very serious look on his face.

"Before we start, we need to do a little talking," he said. "There were some signs that went up today about freeing our animals. First off, if you want to talk about a problem, just come to me. No need to put up signs anonymously."

"Anonymous" was the funny name people called themselves when they didn't want to give out their real names.

"It's a good issue to discuss," he said. "So let me say this: We're hoping to release Lovey, but only when she's completely healed. Jake has been our camp mascot for a while, but I'd be happy to see how you all feel about releasing him."

I gulped hard. It sounded like Hap Holloway was in favor of letting us all go wild. My whiskers twitched as I listened intently.

"As for Og and Humphrey, they are pets. They are not to be released into the wild. They are only on loan to us. Understand?" He waited and there was an uproar from the crowd.

Half of them were chanting, "Hum-phree! Hum-phree! Hum-phree!"

The other half chanted, "Og-Og-Og-Og-Og!"

Noah wasn't chanting. He was just watching the other campers, looking surprised.

The noise was deafening—until Mrs. Wright gave a mighty blow on her whistle.

"There *will be order*!" she exclaimed.

And there was, because the skits began.

The Blue Jays got the show off to a great start. A.J. started this one by coming out onstage, intently looking down at the floor. Aldo came out and asked him what he was doing.

"I'm trying to figure out what kind of tracks these are," A.J. answered loudly, pointing at the ground.

Aldo said, "They look like wolf tracks to me."

Then Simon came in and asked Aldo and A.J. what they were doing. When they explained, Simon said, "They look like bear tracks to me."

Brad came in and asked what they were doing and said, "They look like badger tracks to me."

This went on a few times with the other Blue Jays until A.J. came rushing in again and said, "You guys! Those are *train tracks*!"

Suddenly Richie came in, leading Ms. Mac, Aldo and Maria and even Mrs. Wright directly toward the rest of the boys. They were hanging on to each other's waists, huffing and puffing, tooting and chugging—yes, Mrs. Wright blew her whistle—like a real train while the Blue Jays ran off screaming.

The skit was a hit! I laughed and cheered and so did the others.

I was so HAPPY-HAPPY-HAPPY for the Blue Jays, I almost forgot that I would have to be out there soon.

～•～

The Chickadees came next. One by one, they joined Abby, who was standing with her legs deeply bent, just as they'd look if she were sitting on a real bench. (There was no bench, but they did a good job of pretending to sit on one.)

Once all the girls were sitting on the "bench," Maria came strolling by and asked them what they were doing.

"We're sitting on this invisible bench," Marissa answered.

"Oh," Maria said. Then she pointed to the other side of the stage. "But I moved it over there yesterday."

With that, the Chickadees all tumbled to the floor, while the crowd laughed and clapped. I clapped, too.

Next up were the Bobwhites. They all appeared on-stage holding balloons. Super-Sam came out and directed them like an orchestra conductor. All together, they let the air out of their balloons a little at a time and—you won't believe it—it sounded just like the song "Jingle Bells"! It was such a silly sound, the crowd laughed so loud you could hardly hear the end of the song! When it was finished, they all took deep bows.

I was cheering, too, until Miranda came and whisked my cage off the table—a little roughly, I must say.

"Bye, Og! Enjoy the show!" I squeaked to my friend.

Ms. Mac and the other Robins were setting up a stand-alone door on the stage with the curtains on either side of it while Miranda put my cage directly behind it.

"Okay, Humphrey," Miranda said in a calming voice. "It's showtime. You know what to do."

I was all alone in the middle of the stage (although no one could see me—yet).

The skit began as Kayla came up to the door and opened it partway. Then she slammed it shut and immediately began running around the stage screaming, "Help! Help!"

Lindsey ran onstage and asked her what was wrong.

"There's a monster behind the door! A big scary monster!" she yelled.

"No way," said Lindsey. Then she opened the door, shut it again and began running around the stage shouting, "Help! Help!"

When Miranda came out and asked what was wrong, Lindsey described the monster's glowing eyes, red fangs and ugly face. Then she asked if anybody was brave enough to take a look at it.

Gail was next. She took one look, screamed and ran away. Oh, she was a good screamer, too.

The rest of the Robins did the same.

My ears were twitching from all that screaming and I was feeling a little itchy and twitchy.

Finally, Kayla addressed the audience. "Is anyone out there brave enough to look behind the door?" she asked.

Ms. Mac stood up. (This was all arranged ahead of time, I have to admit.)

"I will," she said. Then she came up onstage, opened the door wide and jumped back, screaming.

At the same time, Miranda came from behind me and pushed my cage out onto the stage so everyone could see me.

"A monster! A monster!" she screamed, running around the stage. She acted really scared.

There I was, on the big stage with all the campers watching. As soon as everyone saw me, they smiled and started laughing, because they knew *I* was no monster.

"Eek!" I said, though I'm not sure how well my voice carried, especially over all the applause.

"Hum-phree! Hum-phree! Hum-phree!" everyone shouted.

The Robins all came out onstage and took a bow. They looked so proud. Gail had the biggest smile of all. She hadn't sniffled in a long time.

My heart was still pounding when Miranda put me back on the table.

"Thanks for saving us, Humphrey," she said. Her eyes were sparkling and her cheeks were pink.

"Anytime," I answered. And I meant it.

When she was gone, I turned to my neighbor.

"How'd I do, Og?" I asked.

Og made an impressive dive to the bottom of his cage, then came out of the water, up on his rock and twanged, "BOING-BOING-BOING!"

It was better than any applause.

Then the older campers put on their skits and did some funny songs, too.

It was hilarious . . . and it lasted way more than an hour!

That night, I stayed with the Bobwhites. They were still playing crazy songs with their balloons.

Once lights were out for the night, they talked a little bit in the dark about Haunted Hollow.

"Do you really think we'll get to see the Howler?" Richie asked.

"It's a cinch," said Sam. "I've got you covered in volleyball, canoeing, swimming and archery."

"You can handle the outdoor skills, can't you, Noah?" Garth asked.

Noah's mind seemed to be far, far away. "Huh? Oh, sure. I know a lot about that stuff."

"Bobwhites forever!" said Garth.

"Bobwhites forever!" the other boys chimed in.

I squeaked along with them, but by now, I really didn't know who to root for.

~·~

The next morning, right before breakfast, Sayeh slipped into the rec room to visit Og and me.

"I am very tired today," she told us. "Last night Abby marked up the whole cabin with twigs and rocks so we could practice reading trail markings. We even got in trouble for keeping our lights on too late." Sayeh sighed. "That won't help our camp spirit score."

"MY-MY-MY." I couldn't think of anything else to say. Here I'd been listening to funny balloon music while Sayeh had to work late!

"I tell you, Humphrey, I like Camp Happy Hollow very much, but I'll be glad when the Clash of the Cabins is over so we can relax and have fun," she said.

Suddenly, a deep voice spoke. "What's this? An unhappy camper?"

It was Hap Holloway. He'd been standing at the door, listening.

Sayeh jumped when she heard him, but when she

turned to look at him, he had a friendly smile on his face.

"I'm always looking for ways to make Camp Happy Hollow a happier place," he said. "It sounds like you might have some good ideas, Sayeh. Why don't you come to my office and we'll talk for a few minutes?"

Sayeh looked down at the floor. I was hoping for her sake that she didn't cry.

"You'll be doing me a favor," Hap said in a softer voice.

"Okay," Sayeh said. "If it will help you."

Then she followed Hap out of the rec room. I watched her through the window, following him up to a cabin where he and the counselors had an office.

She glanced back at me once and I gave her a wave of my paw.

"Good luck, Sayeh," I said, wishing with all my heart she could hear me.

**NOTE TO SELF:** An hour of comedy is FUN-FUN-FUN, but laughs don't always last.

# The Case of the Missing Frog

I kept my eyes fixed on the office building, but it was a long time before I saw Sayeh leave again. Even from a distance, I could see that she was smiling! And she gave a happy wave to Hap Holloway as she skipped back down the path.

How I wished I could have heard their conversation!

At last, it was a peaceful day. Sayeh was still smiling the next time I saw her, and Brad and Gail both seemed more relaxed. Brad talked to lots of people now and so did Gail. Who would have thought a couple of stickers could do that much good?

Garth and the Bobwhites were brimming with confidence that they would be spending the night at Haunted Hollow, and who would doubt it, with Super-Sam on their team? But Abby and the Chickadees stood strong and tall and still thought they had a chance.

Miranda and the other Robins were more relaxed, too, since their skit had gone over well.

I thought maybe it was time for me to kick back and

just enjoy camp. I was so relaxed, I took a nice long doze while my friends were off on their hike.

But I was wide awake when Ms. Mac made an announcement at the end of the session. "Tomorrow we start two days of competitions to cap the Clash of the Cabins competition. The nature quizzes will be tomorrow, for anyone who wants to take them," she said. "Good luck, campers, and have a great time!"

I felt a little shiver of excitement but also uneasiness. So soon? I thought. Were my friends ready? Was I ready?

I hopped on my wheel to relieve my anxiety. It didn't work.

I spent that night with the Blue Jays, but they left for a while to go to the evening campfire. I wasn't sure what was special about campfire nights, but my friends were always keyed up when they came back.

"I've just got to see that Howler," A.J. said. "It would be awful if my little brother, Ty, got to see him and I didn't."

"We've got a good shot," Richie said.

"Yeah. Blue Jays rule!" That was Brad, and whether or not the Blue Jays got to spend the night in Haunted Hollow, he was still a winner in my book.

Richie took me down to the rec room the next morning. I was there before Og, but I didn't think anything of it at first. I was busy watching my friends streaming into Happy Hollow Hall, chattering away.

Og still wasn't there by the time breakfast began. I was puzzled, but I was also interested in how the whole atmosphere of camp had changed. While the kids in different cabins often hung out together during their free time, I noticed that today the campers who shared cabins stuck together.

The place just *sounded* different.

"Bob-whites! Bob-whites!" came the call from one table.

"Chick-a-chick-a-chickadees!" came from another.

A.J. led his cabin's "Blue Jays rule!" chant.

"Robins! Robins! Rah-rah-rah!" was followed by a lot of giggling.

I heard it all, but Og didn't. Because Og had never arrived.

"Maybe somebody already took him over to the Nature Center," Ms. Mac said as she carried my cage down the path after breakfast. Sure, somebody took him over to the Nature Center, I figured. But who?

As soon as we entered, I knew something was VERY-VERY-VERY wrong. Og's tank was there all right . . . but Og wasn't in it. I could see right away that he hadn't popped the top himself, because it was firmly in place.

Lovey, who was usually calm and quiet, was flapping her wings and making excited sounds. Even Jake wiggled more than usual.

Ms. Mac set my cage down and checked the tank to make sure Og wasn't hiding behind a plant.

Some of the campers were gathering to take their nature quizzes. Ms. Mac asked them if they'd seen Og, but no one had.

Katie came in and she was pretty upset at the news. She organized the kids and they searched every inch of the room, under chairs and in potted plants.

"Og! Where are you!" I squeaked at the top of my lungs. "Og! Come out! We're worried!"

I waited to hear a friendly "BOING-BOING," but it didn't come.

The rest of the morning was a blur. The very loud bell rang to call all the campers to the dining hall. Thank goodness, Ms. Mac took me, too.

Once everyone was gathered, Hap Holloway got up onstage and explained that Og was missing. That caused quite a stir. I thought Miranda was going to cry!

Hap asked if anyone knew what had happened to him.

There was a lot of shuffling and whispering. Finally, Noah stood up.

"I know," he said.

You can bet that all eyes were on Noah. He didn't seem very happy about it.

"Where *is* he?" I screeched.

Hap motioned for him to come up to the stage. "Come on up here, Noah, and tell me."

Noah slowly made his way to the stage.

"Well," he said, "sometimes I get up early and go down to the lake. I guess that's against the rules, but it's beautiful at that time of day. The birds sing more then and I even saw some deer one morning."

Hap nodded. "We'll discuss that later. So what happened?"

"I was sitting on the shore and watching these frogs swimming and hopping in the shallow water. They looked so happy, I thought Og might like to meet some other frogs and play in a real lake," he explained. "So I came back to our cabin and I borrowed him. Everybody was sleeping."

"And you let him go at the lake?" Hap asked.

Noah looked a little frightened. "No, I didn't mean to! I just thought I'd let him play there awhile. But as soon as I put him down, he hopped off into some tall grass and disappeared. I looked and looked, but I couldn't find him."

There was a lot of commotion among the unhappy campers. No one was as unhappy as me.

"So I just took his tank over to the Nature Center," Noah continued. "I didn't know what to do."

"You should have told us," Hap said. "It's not easy for pets that are used to being fed to find their own food." He sounded firm but kind.

Noah hung his head. "I'm really sorry. I looked for him, honest."

The noise in the dining hall had grown to an uproar.

Then it came, that ear-piercing blast of a whistle. Mrs. Wright joined Hap on the stage.

"Do you know where you left him, young man?" she asked Noah in a voice that wasn't as kind as Hap's.

Noah nodded.

"We should organize a search party," she announced. "You can take us down to the spot you last saw him. All right with you, Holloway?"

"It's all right with me!" I squeaked. "Great idea!"

And I thought Mrs. Wright didn't like Og! I guess I judged another book by its cover.

There wasn't much Hap could do except agree with her. He nodded and soon the counselors were organizing the campers into groups. They gathered up nets and buckets, sunscreen and caps, and Noah and Mrs. Wright led them out of the hall.

"Sam will find him," I heard Garth tell Simon. "He can do anything."

I hoped he was right.

Just as I feared, they left me behind. Ms. Mac took me to the rec room and told me not to worry. But she didn't tell me *how*.

I nervously peered out the window for hours and hours and hours. Maria came in from the kitchen once and gave me some lovely veggies, but I couldn't think of eating until my old friend was safely back in his tank.

～⌣～

When they returned from lunch, I could tell by the faces of the searchers that they hadn't found Og. The dining hall was a lot quieter than usual.

After lunch, Hap Holloway had the kids vote to decide if they wanted to go back and look some more.
Apparently, they all did.

Before they left, they sang the Camp Happy Hollow
song.

I tried to sing along, but a big lump in my throat
made it unsqueakably difficult.

～⌣～

The afternoon seemed to go on forever, and when the
campers returned, they still weren't smiling.

Ms. Mac came in the rec room and pulled up a chair
next to my cage.

"Humphrey, we didn't find him. I'm sure he'll be fine
there in the lake with the other frogs," she said. Her eyes
looked all wet. "But I know he misses you as much as
you miss him."

Sayeh and Miranda came in, arm in arm.

"May we see Humphrey, please?" Miranda asked.

"Sure," Ms. Mac said.

"I'm sorry, Humphrey," Miranda finally said. "We really tried. I looked so hard, my eyeballs hurt."

"We're going back tomorrow," Sayeh said. "I'm never
giving up. Never."

"Thank you," I squeaked weakly.

For the first time in my short life, my cage felt like a
prison.

～⌣～

"I'm never giving up," Sayeh had said.

I heard those words in my head all evening. And after

I was safely in the Robins' Nest that night, I kept hearing them. My friends had given their all looking for Og and I hadn't done one single thing!

I was mad at myself and sorry for myself all at once. I was mad at Noah and sorry for him, too. And then I heard it:

SKITTER-SKITTER-SKITTER.

SCRITCH-SCRITCH-SCRITCH.

Goldenrod was under the cabin again. I didn't think twice about what I had to do. I slid down the table leg and found an opening between the floorboards.

"Goldenrod? It's Humphrey," I squeaked.

"Hi, Humphrey! What are you doing out of your cage?" she squeaked back.

"I need your help," I said. "I'll meet you outside."

I scampered to the door. There was a nice wide opening between the bottom of the door and the floor and I easily slid through it. When I got out to the porch, I saw Goldenrod waiting in a clump of bushes.

I was so excited, I probably didn't make sense, but I told her about Og and what had happened.

"Maybe he wants to be wild," Goldenrod said.

"Maybe," I agreed. "But I have to know for myself."

Goldenrod thought for a moment. "I'll help you, but it's a long way to the lake. Oh, wait—I know a shortcut."

Soon, I found myself following Goldenrod down the path in the moonlight. Then she veered off the path, into thick underbrush—almost like the jungle I'd seen in that movie back in the library. Longfellow School seemed a million, jillion miles away.

I was out in the wild, like the lions and gorillas and hootie owls.

It was SCARY-SCARY-SCARY. It was also *thrilling*.

**NOTE TO SELF:** Always help a friend in trouble ... or at least try.

# Moonlight Rescue

Goldenrod moved quickly through the brush. I was right behind her, but oh, the grass and branches and tiny rocks tickled my whiskers, scraped my paws and made me itchy all over.

SKITTER-SKATTER-SKIT.

There was someone else in the brush. Could it be the Howler?

SKITTER-SKATTER-SQUEAK.

I was pretty sure the Howler didn't squeak.

"Come on, Lucky," Goldenrod said. "We have to help our friend Humphrey."

Then I heard SQUEAK-SKITTER-SKAT.

"You can help too, Go-Go," she said.

Soon, there were about a dozen mice accompanying us, Goldenrod's brothers, sisters and cousins. They scampered along through the underbrush as I desperately tried to keep up.

Then I heard HOOT-HOOT. HOOT-HOOT.

"Excuse me," I said, gasping a bit for air. "But did I just hear an *owl*?"

"Sure," said Goldenrod. "That's why we try not to go out in the open."

"Good call," I agreed.

And then I saw the most wonderful sight I'd ever seen. The moonlight shimmered and glimmered across the surface of the lake. The water was silvery-purple. I guess that's why it was called Lake Lavender. It was beautiful.

Oh, but I also felt a bad feeling deep in my tummy. Maybe Og would prefer this beautiful lake to his table-top tank. Maybe Og was happier with the frogs in Lake Lavender than he was living next door to a hamster.

Goldenrod led us to the very edge of the water, where there were tall plants and soft grasses.

"Here we are," she squeaked. At least I think that's what she squeaked. I could barely hear her over the deafening chorus of frogs!

I never knew there were so many kinds of frogs and so many different sounds.

QUANK-QUANK-QUANK!

RUMM-RUMM-RUMM!

TUCK-A-TUCK-A-TUCK!

CHIRP-CHIRP-CHIRP!

But I didn't hear a single BOING.

"How can I find him?" I asked Goldenrod.

"Call him," she said. "Maybe he'll hear you."

There was a nice flat rock nearby. I climbed up to the top, cleared my throat and squeaked with all my might.

"Og? This is your friend Humphrey! Og? Og!"

The quanking and chirping continued. If only those big bullfrogs would stop RUMM-RUMM-RUMM-ing for a second.

"OG!" I shrieked. "OG, IT'S HUMPHREY!"

Oddly enough, the chorus suddenly became quiet, quiet enough for me to hear a clear and distinct "BOING!" I'd know that BOING anywhere.

"Og, if you'd rather stay here at the lake where it's beautiful in the moonlight, I'll understand," I told him. "But if you'd like to come back and be my neighbor again, we can lead you back."

"BOING-BOING!" was the response.

"My friends know the way," I continued. "And the kids miss you a lot."

"BOING-BOING-BOING!"

Did that sound a little bit closer?

"I'm here, on a rock on the shore," I told him. I was afraid my small hamster voice might not hold up much longer.

"BOING-BOING," Og answered.

I waited and waited until I heard a familiar splashing. And then I saw him: his bright green skin shining in the moonlight, his big googly eyes gleaming and that big old goofy grin. He was on shore, hopping toward me.

"Og! I missed you!" I shouted.

"BOING-BOING!" he replied, so I knew he'd missed me, too.

HOOT-HOOT. HOOT-HOOT.

"Hurry, let's get back in the brush," Goldenrod said.

Quietly, without another squeak, Goldenrod, Lucky, Go-Go and others led Og and me skittering and hopping through the undergrowth on the long trek back to the Robins' Nest cabin.

"I can't thank you all enough," I told my wild friends.

They squeaked, "Good luck," and scampered off, disappearing into the bushes.

Only Goldenrod lingered for a few seconds.

"You are a wonderful friend to Og," she told me.

"*You* are a wonderful friend to *me*," I replied. "And Goldenrod? You'll be careful with that owl, won't you?"

"Of course," she said. "But Lucky can tell you more about that owl than I can. He was just a baby when an owl swooped down and picked him up."

I gasped, "Oh, no!"

Goldenrod nodded. "But for some reason, he dropped him right away. That's how he got his name—Lucky."

I shuddered a little and she turned to leave.

"If I EVER-EVER-EVER can help you, please let me know," I called after her.

"Thanks," she said shyly. Then, in a flash, she was gone.

꧁◦◦꧂

I looked over at my old pal, who looked tired and pale. Of course—he needed water! Luckily, there was a lovely puddle at the bottom of the steps. After sitting in the water awhile, he looked like his old self again.

I sat there with Og for the rest of the night. Neither of us said a thing. We didn't need to.

When it started to get light, I told Og to stay right where he was. Then I slid back under the door.

I knew from experience that there was no way to get back on the table, so I waited. When the loudspeaker played that awful wake-up song, the girls began to stir.

As soon as I saw Miranda sit up, I began to SQUEAK-SQUEAK-SQUEAK at the top of my lungs. She heard me and jumped out of bed.

"Humphrey! You're out of your cage!" she said, dashing toward me.

I was way ahead of her. I raced to the door and slid under.

"Come back!" Miranda ran after me and opened the door.

I hurried down to Og's puddle. He was still there, thank goodness.

Miranda stopped short and stared. "Og! That's Og!" she screamed.

The other Robins were outside now, screaming with happiness. Gail picked up my cage first and then Og.

"I'll go tell Ms. Mac." Miranda took off running, still in her pj's!

～⌒～

"Tell me again," Ms. Mac said after Og was back in his tank and I was back in my cage.

Miranda told the story again.

"I'm afraid with all the fuss about Og, one of you forgot to lock Humphrey's cage," she said.

"Sorry," the Robins said in unison.

I felt a little guilty because they didn't have anything to be sorry about.

Ms. Mac pointed a finger in my direction. "And you, Humphrey, were naughty to get out of your cage."

Naughty, yes. But it was well worth it to have my friend back.

"I guess somehow Og found his way back, though I can't imagine how," Ms. Mac continued. "But here he is and that's all that counts."

I couldn't have agreed more.

⌒⌒

Og and I put in a special appearance in the dining hall at breakfast that morning to loud cheers and applause.

Noah got up and apologized to Og and to the other campers. I could tell he was REALLY-REALLY-REALLY sorry.

"I thought I knew a lot about animals," he said. "I thought that frogs belonged with frogs. But now I know some frogs belong with people."

Then Hap prepared everyone for the final day of competitions.

"Play hard, play fair, have fun," he said. "And now, let the games begin!"

I glanced over at Sayeh. This was the moment she'd been dreading.

Surprise—she had a big smile on her face! Humans are hard to figure out. But that's what makes them so interesting.

**NOTE TO SELF:** You can know-a-lot. But nobody knows everything.

## The Winners After Dinner

⌒⌒⌒⌒⌒⌒⌒⌒⌒⌒⌒⌒⌒⌒

**W**ait up, Garth!" Sam was standing right in front of my cage.

Garth hurried over. "What's the matter? Your pitching arm's okay, isn't it?"

At that moment, Sam was using his pitching arm to scratch his other arm. And then his neck. And then his leg.

"I'm itching like crazy," he said. "I can hardly stand it."

Garth's jaw dropped open as he stared at Super-Sam, who now could be called Scratching Sam. His skin was red and bumpy and blistery, and just watching Sam scratch made me itch.

A small crowd gathered around Sam.

"I'll get the nurse," Richie said, and he took off running.

⌒⌒⌒

Nurse Rose took one look at Sam. "Poison ivy," she said. "Come with me."

Still scratching and looking completely miserable,

Sam followed her to the infirmary, where the sick kids stayed.

"We're toast!" Garth told Ty. "The Bobwhites are toast!"

⌒⌒

I spent my day with Og (and Lovey and Jake) in the Nature Center, where kids came and went all day to take the nature test. Katie stayed in the center, while Ms. Mac was out on the trail, timing the groups for the trail-reading event.

It wasn't an easy day.

Part of me wished I could be out there, free of my cage, watching the events and seeing how my friends were doing.

The other part of me remembered that it was dangerous for a small creature to be out in the big woods. In fact, I worried about Goldenrod and her friends every night.

Still, I was anxious to know what was going on. I kept my eyes and ears open for any little tidbits to tell me how the competitions were going.

The first thing I heard was from Garth, when he came in to take the quiz. He looked miserable.

"Nurse Rose gave Sam some lotion, but she says he can't swim," Garth told me. "He can try canoeing or softball, but I don't see how he can hit a home run when he's scratching all the time. The other teams say he shouldn't play volleyball because they don't want to touch the ball after he does." Garth sighed. "I don't think he can do anything but scratch."

"I'm SORRY-SORRY-SORRY," I told him, knowing he and the Bobwhites had all counted on Sam to win for them. Maybe Sam's cabin-mates should have put forth a little more effort, but I was too polite to say so, especially when Garth was upset.

Sayeh was a lot more chipper than Garth when she stopped by after taking the nature quiz.

"Oh, Humphrey," she said. "No one can tie knots like Abby, though Simon did a good job. Marissa's ahead in archery. We're going trail reading now. But even if the Chickadees don't win, we'll still have a great time tomorrow night."

I was GLAD-GLAD-GLAD she felt that way!

The next night was when the winning group would sleep over in Haunted Hollow. But how would the Chickadees have a great time if they didn't get to go?

Sayeh walked away but quickly returned.

"Oh, I forgot," she said. "Miranda was awesome in volleyball, so the Robins are still in the game. I'm so happy for her."

I was happy for Miranda *and* Sayeh.

Brad took the nature quiz and I could tell he worked really hard at it. He practically chewed right through his pencil, which would be easy for a hamster but not so easy for a human. When the quiz was over, he called for Gail to wait up.

"A.J. hit a home run," he said. "Even if we don't win, it was close."

"I'm sure you did well on the nature quiz," Gail said. "And my goofy brother was pretty good at tying knots. Who knew?"

"Did you hear that hammering noise?" he asked.

Then they wandered off, talking about woodpeckers, which are interesting birds, but they make way too much noise for the sensitive ears of a small furry creature like me!

"Og, have you been keeping track?" I asked. "Because I've been listening all day and I can't tell who's going to win. Can you?"

Og just sat there. I guess he was still trying to figure it out, too.

◦~◦

When they are nervous, humans bite their fingernails or pace the floor.

When I am nervous, I hop on my wheel. (By the way, I don't think biting your fingers or paws is a good idea.)

So I gave my old wheel a good spin later in the day, when we were back in the rec room. The counselors had gathered there with clipboards and all kinds of papers. They were going to decide who would spend the night in Haunted Hollow—and they were deciding it right in front of me.

"No doubt about it. The Bobwhites would have won

147

if Sam didn't have poison ivy," Aldo said, staring at his clipboard.

"I feel for them," Hap Holloway agreed. "It was a bad piece of luck."

"Still, the others had been slacking off," Mrs. Wright observed. "I think they relied too much on Sam. And their scores just don't add up."

The others agreed with Mrs. Wright and amazingly, so did I! Really, she wasn't so bad, if she'd just lose that whistle!

Katie rummaged through her papers and chuckled. "I've never seen anyone tie knots like Abby. She racked up points for the Chickadees on that one. And on trail reading. And Marissa won archery."

Ms. Mac nodded. "But the Robins had a lot of heart, and Miranda and Gail got second in canoeing. And Lindsey was a big surprise with her volleyball serves."

Aldo studied his clipboard some more. "A.J. and Simon took the top spots in swimming. And Brad won the canoeing and scored very close to Sayeh on the nature quiz. I think the Blue Jays' scores are the highest."

Hap Holloway was busily adding up scores. "Yep," he said. "It's the Blue Jays."

Katie shook her head. "I guess there'll be a lot of disappointed kids, especially when they don't get to go to Haunted Hollow."

"Not necessarily," Hap said. "No, I don't think they'll be disappointed tomorrow night, thanks to Sayeh."

I had no idea what Hap was talking about.

I was worried about my friends being disappointed when Aldo brought Og and me into the dining hall that night so we could hear the results.

First, Hap congratulated everyone on being great campers.

Then he announced the rankings. There was a lot of cheering when he said that the Robins came in third. There was more cheering when Hap said that the Bob-whites and Chickadees *tied* for second place.

When the room quieted down, Hap said, "And in first place, the winners of this year's Clash of the Cabins competition: the Blue Jays!"

"Blue Jays rule!" A.J. and his cabin-mates chanted.

"Blue Jays rule!" I happily squeaked along.

After the cheering ended, Hap continued. "I have to recognize one camper as being one of the most outstanding athletes I've ever seen at this camp." Hap paused. "That's Sam Gorman. Today's scores might have turned out differently if it weren't for that poison ivy. So let's give Sam a big Happy Hollow cheer."

Everybody cheered—even Og and me. Sam stood up and waved, but I still felt itchy just looking at him.

And wonder of wonders, afterward the campers all mingled and were friendly again. A few looked disappointed, but Abby, Miranda and Sayeh chatted away as if nothing had ever happened. And I was happy to see that Brad and Richie were hanging out with Noah.

Humans are pretty amazing. I was sorry Goldenrod didn't know how VERY-VERY-VERY nice they can be.

That night, I slept in the cabin shared by Ms. Mac, Katie and Mrs. Wright. (Believe it or not, she took off her whistle before she went to bed—but she placed it right under her pillow.)

Still, it was a quiet night and everyone slept well.

Everyone except me.

Because all I could think of that night was what would happen the next night.

The night the Blue Jays would go to Haunted Hollow.

**NOTE TO SELF:** Winning is good, but not winning isn't as bad as most humans imagine.

## Happy Day, Haunted Night

The next day, it was difficult for the Blue Jays to think of anything except their upcoming night with the Howler.

Even if they forgot about it for a few minutes, the other campers would come up to them and go, "Owoooo! Owoooo!"

In fact, they did it so often, I think the Blue Jays were having second thoughts about spending the night in Haunted Hollow at all.

In the Nature Center, however, there was a lot going on. During the first session in the morning, Katie and Ms. Mac brought in a stranger—a very nice stranger, as it turned out. He was Dr. Singleton, the veterinarian from the wildlife refuge who had helped Katie with Lovey's wing when she was first rescued.

"Dr. Singleton's here to see if Lovey's healed enough to be released," Ms. Mac explained.

The vet was a big, tall man with a full black beard. But he was as gentle as he was big and was a real expert on birds.

While the kids in the first session watched, he examined Lovey carefully.

"She looks completely healed," he said. "And I imagine she's getting a little tired of her crate."

Her crate was rather plain compared to my cage. She didn't have any fun things to play with, like I do.

"I think we could try her out today," he said.

Katie looked at her watch. "It's almost time for a break between sessions. I'll make an announcement."

Dr. Singleton stayed and answered questions while she went down to the office.

Then Ms. Mac introduced him to Og and me.

"You're a fine specimen," he said to me. "I don't think you need my help at all."

I hopped on my wheel to show him he was right.

"Ah, *Rana clamitans,*" he said to Og.

"No, his name is Og!" I squeaked, but he didn't understand me.

"I guess you kids are used to his interesting twang," he said.

After living next to Og for months, I was very used to it.

Then Dr. Singleton turned his attention to Jake the Snake. "How did you end up in a cage?" he asked Jake.

Jake stuck his tongue out, as usual. How rude!

Then we heard Katie on the LOUD-LOUD-LOUD-SPEAKER.

"Attention, campers," her voice boomed. "We are

going to try to release Lovey into the wild after this session. Anyone who wants to participate, come directly to the Nature Center."

Within minutes, there was a rush, a dash, no—a *stampede*—to the Nature Center as every single camper showed up. Ms. Mac made them form a half circle in front of the building.

Then she asked Sayeh, Brad and Noah to be her assistants. (They had scored the highest on the quiz.)

Miranda picked up my cage so I could watch—what a thoughtful girl!

Brad and Noah carried out Lovey Dovey's crate. Her head poked up out of the top as she watched everyone and everything.

Then Dr. Singleton carefully lifted Lovey out of the crate and showed Sayeh how to hold her.

Sayeh held Lovey just the way he showed her and looked completely confident.

"First, put her down on the porch and let her try her wings," the vet told her.

When Lovey touched the ground, the first thing she did was spread her wings. I couldn't even tell which one had been injured.

Then she flapped her wings and hopped, as if ready for takeoff.

The kids in the crowd stayed pretty quiet, as they'd been instructed, but they couldn't help "oohing" and "aahing" a little. Neither could I.

"That's great," Dr. Singleton said. "That hopping means she's ready to fly. But we need a big open space. Pick her up again, Sayeh, if you can."

Then he had her take Lovey up the hill to the spot where I'd viewed the two hollows. It was a high open meadow surrounded by trees. The other campers—and Miranda carrying my cage—followed quietly.

It was time for Sayeh to put her on the ground and see if she flew. But at the last minute, Sayeh didn't do it.

Instead, she turned to Noah and handed Lovey over. "Here, Noah, I think you should do this," she said.

That was just about the nicest thing I'd ever seen a human do.

I held my breath as Noah set her on the ground.

And then, with no further encouragement, she flapped her wings and took off, flying up to a very high treetop in the distance.

The crowd couldn't stay quiet any longer. They let out a cheer.

Dr. Singleton looked as pleased as Katie and Ms. Mac.

"She knew just what to do," he said. "You all did a great job with her. Keep an eye out for her for a while, but I don't think there'll be a problem."

Just then, Lovey flew away from the tree and circled right over the Nature Center. We watched her until she flew out of sight.

"Any questions?" Katie asked while we were still in the meadow.

Noah slowly raised his hand. "I was just wondering . . . what about the snake?"

Dr. Singleton nodded. "I was thinking about him, too. He looked a little confined to me. How would you feel about releasing him?"

Katie and Ms. Mac looked out at the campers.

"Should we take a vote?" Ms. Mac asked.

They hardly needed a vote at all. Just about everybody thought Jake would be happier outside of his cage.

This time, Brad was the one who got to let him out of his cage. It didn't take long for Jake to slither away and disappear in the grass.

Again, the crowd cheered.

"Boy," I heard Brad say. "Nothing like this ever happened at my old camp."

It was a thrilling sight, seeing Lovey and Jake go free. I only hoped I wouldn't be next!

But I had nothing to fear. The session was over and I was returned to the Nature Center. It was a little lonely there without Lovey and I even missed Jake (a little). But at least I had my friend, *Rana clamitans,* to keep me company. Who ever knew that a little frog had such a fancy name!

All of the excitement at the Nature Center had taken my mind off of Haunted Hollow—at least for a little while.

In fact, I was so relaxed, I settled in for a long doze in the rec room.

Ms. Mac came in to check on Og and me. She told me that she was taking all the campers except the Blue Jays to the nearest town to see a movie. "See you later," she said. Then she winked at me. I had no idea why.

I managed to doze off again, but I was awakened abruptly when I heard pounding footsteps racing toward me.

"Humphrey Dumpty!" A.J. shouted excitedly. "You're coming with us to Haunted Hollow!"

"Who, me?" I was astounded.

"Yep, Hap Holloway said it was okay as long as we make sure your cage is locked at all times and keep you in our tent," he explained. "We didn't want you to miss out."

There are some things I wouldn't mind missing out on and the Howler was one of them. But A.J. was already holding my cage and hurrying back to the dining hall.

"It's been nice knowing you, Og!" I called back to my friend. There wasn't even time to say good-bye.

~·~·~

It was dark outside. Instead of hiking in the dark, Hap took us all in a small bus and drove us what seemed like a LONG-LONG-LONG way from Camp Happy Hollow. Even though Haunted Hollow was next door to our camp, to get there, we had to drive on a road that wound round and round a hill.

"Blue Jays," he said as he drove. "You are about to join a small but special group of campers. Few have earned the right to go to Haunted Hollow. But none will ever forget . . . the Howler!"

He opened his mouth wide and let out the most spine-tingling "owoooo!" I'd heard yet. I dove under my bedding, just in case Hap really *was* the Howler.

At last, the bus stopped and Hap let us out. It was still quite a hike to the campground, where Aldo was waiting. Several tents had been set up and a fire was blazing in a big stone pit. The flames cast orange and yellow shadows, like huge fingers, on the nearby trees.

"Welcome to Haunted Hollow," Aldo said. Somehow, he didn't seem as jolly and carefree as usual. "Take a seat."

The Blue Jays sat on big rocks around the campfire. A.J. put my cage next to his feet and I could feel the heat from the fire. As far as I was concerned, I was a little too close for comfort. And even though my friends had waited a long time for this night, they were suddenly unusually quiet.

As I glanced over at the dense brush nearby, I thought I saw some eyes—maybe the friendly eyes of Goldenrod and her friends watching these strange humans. I hoped they were the *only* wild creatures hanging around.

Hap stood near the fire and addressed the campers. Like Aldo, he was acting very serious.

"Boys, you are about to share in the secret of Haunted Hollow," he began. "Twenty years ago, I bought this camp. The man I bought it from didn't want to sell it, but he ran out of money and had no choice."

157

The strange shadows made Hap's face and hair even redder than usual.

"He was a crazy kind of fellow, with white hair to his shoulders and a white beard to his waist. On the day he signed the papers to hand the land over to me, he said, 'It will never truly be yours, Holloway. For I will haunt this land as long as I live . . . and even after!'"

The boys gasped and I accidentally let out an "eeek!"

"I tore down his small cabin that was on this spot. But once a year, the best campers are chosen to come here to show him that even if the place is haunted, *we are not afraid*," he continued.

"My cousin saw him last year," Richie said, his eyes wide.

Hap nodded. "So far, the Howler has shown up every year. But this year, who knows? So I want you all to shout with me, 'We are not afraid! We are not afraid!'"

The Blue Jays didn't exactly shout at first, but they joined in.

"We are not afraid! We are not afraid!"

I joined in, too, as the voices got louder and louder.

"We are not afraid! We are not afraid!"

Then they got more confident . . . and the volume increased.

*"We are not afraid! We are not afraid!"*

And then, it happened. A howl so loud, so hideous, so unsqueakably scary, I think my heart stopped beating.

"OWOOOO! OWOOO!"

No one human could possibly make a noise that loud.

The noise grew closer and there was a rustling in the grass.

"OWOOOO! OWOOO!"

The Blue Jays all jumped up, screaming, and started running around in circles.

"OWOOOO! OWOOO!"

There I was, alone on the ground with the Howler approaching. I closed my eyes.

Then *I felt my cage move!* It had grabbed me!

"Don't worry, Humphrey. I've got you. You're safe," a familiar voice assured me.

It was Aldo.

"OWOOOO! OWOOO!" It was so close now, I thought I heard it breathing. "OWOOOO-OWOOOO— *WE FOOLED YOU!*"

Then there were peals of laughter as out from behind the trees and the bushes came all the other campers: Sayeh, Miranda, Garth, Abby, even itchy Sam! They were pointing and laughing as the Blue Jays stood staring in total confusion.

"What are you doing here?" A.J. said when he saw his brother, Ty, in the crowd.

Hap was laughing harder than anyone. "You want to tell them, Sayeh?" he asked.

Sayeh smiled but shook her head. "You do it, please."

Hap gathered the whole group around the campfire.

"One of the counselors usually comes out here and

howls," he explained. "But when Sayeh explained that she didn't like the idea of so many campers being left out, we cooked up this idea. We figured this was a way for all campers to be part of the legend of the Howler and to have a little fun. What do you think?"

"I was scared to death," Simon said. He looked a little pale.

"I thought I *had* died of fright," Brad added. "But then I saw you guys—pretty funny. You fooled us all right."

"Listen up, folks, this is our secret," Hap explained. "What happened here tonight doesn't get out. We don't want to ruin the surprise for next year's campers, okay?"

Everyone agreed.

I was glad to see that the Blue Jays were good sports about the trick, and the evening continued with lots of songs and toasted marshmallows (which are a little too messy for hamsters) and Aldo even entertained by balancing a broom on one finger for a LONG-LONG-LONG time—my favorite trick!

When it was bedtime, the Blue Jays went to their tents, but the other campers returned to Camp Happy Hollow—and I went with them.

Og and I both slept in Ms. Mac's cabin that night, and even though I'm nocturnal, I slept the whole night through!

**NOTE TO SELF:** I guess it's okay to fib a little (about something like a Howler) as long as it's for FUN!

# The End and the Beginning

The next day was blissful and relaxing. I missed Lovey (and maybe even Jake) in the Nature Center, but when my friends returned from their nature hike, they were very excited because they'd seen Lovey in a tree!

I was quite happy and content and managed to doze all through dinner that night.

Right after dinner, the counselors came into the rec room and woke me up with all their chatter. They behaved in a very peculiar way that night!

First of all, they all put on strange costumes: crazy wigs, false noses, funny hats—they looked SILLY-SILLY-SILLY. Mrs. Wright seemed completely ridiculous, wearing a pink and blue wig and a clown suit! (She kept her whistle, though.)

Nurse Rose was dressed like a little girl with a lollipop.

Ms. Mac and Counselor Katie were dressed like old ladies—which they were not!

They laughed and joked and generally acted more like kids than counselors.

Aldo—wearing an out-of-control white wig, fake

nose, huge glasses and a white coat like doctors wear—carried Og and me into the dining hall.

"You guys won't want to miss this," he said.

The campers roared with laughter when they saw the ridiculous-looking counselors. And they went wild when Hap Holloway came out dressed like the Howler, wearing ragged clothes with a white beard hanging to his waist and long white hair that reached his shoulders.

"It's time for the Counselor's Choice Awards," Hap announced.

Then one by one, they presented the goofiest awards you ever heard of.

Gail, who still loved to giggle, was named the Funniest Camper and A.J. was the Loudest Camper.

"THANKS!" he bellowed when he came onstage to accept his prize: a whoopee cushion, which makes very rude noises.

Miranda received the prize for Most Likely to Become a Counselor. (I'd like to go to her camp someday.)

Sayeh had the Best Smile and Kayla was the Best Sleeper. Abby got a prize for "Knottiest" Camper and everybody cheered.

Naturally, Sam got an award for Itchiest Camper.

Noah got the Nature Lovers award.

Brad was very proud to be Most Improved Camper (which was true) and Simon was happy to be named the Loudest Burper! (An award he deserved.)

The awards went on and on until I think everybody had received something.

Then Hap said there was just one award left: Most Popular. And this year, the counselors couldn't decide, so it was a tie.

I was waiting to hear who the lucky campers were when Ms. Mac picked up my cage and Katie picked up Og's tank and carried us to the stage.

"The winners are Humphrey . . . and Og!" Hap announced.

We received special treats (the best kind—the kind you can eat) and again the crowd went wild.

The noise got so out of control, Mrs. Wright had to use her whistle to quiet things down again.

Suddenly, Hap seemed a lot more serious.

"I have to say, this has been one of the best sessions ever at Camp Happy Hollow," he said. "I learned a lot from all of you. And now that it's about to end, I just hope you'll all be back again next year!"

*Camp was about to end? Just the way school had?*

I wasn't just surprised. I wasn't just sad. I was SICK-SICK-SICK. It was bad enough that school had ended and I wasn't in Room 26 anymore. Now camp was ending, too. Isn't there anything a hamster can count on to last?

When they all sang the Camp Happy Hollow song, I felt so miserable, I just crawled into my sleeping hut, even though I knew I'd never sleep.

I spent that night with the Blue Jays, since they had won the competition for Best All-Around Team.

They exchanged addresses and phone numbers and e-mails and were a little quieter than on the other nights I'd stayed there.

Just before lights-out, A.J. came over to my cage. "Humphrey Dumpty, don't worry. I'm sure we'll see each other again."

I crossed my paws and hoped so. I hoped so all night long.

In the morning, Og and I watched from the rec room window as a line of cars drove up to the camp. Car doors opened and out came moms and dads and little brothers and sisters. Parents and campers carried suitcases, boxes, backpacks and duffel bags from the cabins to the cars.

Some of my friends came in to say good-bye: Miranda and Abby, Ty and A.J. and surprisingly, even Brad. Gail came in by herself and she had gifts for Og and me.

"I made these friendship bracelets in arts and crafts," she said, holding up two colorful woven bands. "I was going to give one to Mom and one to Heidi, but I changed my mind. I'll make new ones for them. I want you to have these."

"THANKS-THANKS-THANKS!" I said, and Og splashed happily.

"I made a lot of new friends here," Gail said as she taped one bracelet to the front of Og's cage and wove the other one in and out of the bars of my cage. "But you'll always be my special friends."

And as she turned to leave, she told us, "I'll tell Heidi hello from you!"

She hurried back outside, and after much hugging and many farewells, doors slammed and the cars pulled away, leaving the camp almost unbearably quiet.

"Was it just a dream, Og?" I asked my neighbor, who was floating lazily in the watery part of his tank. "It went so fast."

He didn't answer. He didn't have to. A camp alive with fun-loving kids wasn't a dream. Now it was a memory.

Later, Ms. Mac came in to check on us.

"Why are you two looking so gloomy?" she asked. "Your work isn't finished yet! Tomorrow a new group of campers arrive for the *next* session of camp."

"What?" I squeaked.

"BOING-BOING!" Og twanged.

Ms. Mac laughed. "Summer's not over yet," she said. "And neither is camp."

That was the BEST-BEST-BEST news I'd heard since the end of school!

The counselors had a quiet dinner in the dining hall. When Og and I were alone again, I looked out at the moonlit camp. If I went to the very top of my cage, I could even see a silvery sliver of Lake Lavender.

"You know what, Og?" I said. "Camp is great because we get to help our friends and have lots of fun."

He splashed gently in response.

"But the best part is, we get to be together," I continued.

Og leaped out of the water and goodness, I thought he'd pop the top of his tank!

"BOING-BOING-BOING-BOING!"

⌣⌣⌣

We stayed alone in the rec room that night, but I really couldn't sleep, because the words of the camp song kept running through my head. And as I sang them softly to myself, I changed the words just a little.

> *Happy Hollow—a place close to my heart.*
> *Happy Hollow—I loved it from the start.*
> *Every day I wake up with so much to do,*
> *Having fun with Og and that Bunny Foo Foo.*
> *I'll remember forever my new friend Goldenrod,*
> *Lovey, too, and Jake, but he is rather odd.*
> *Though I don't know where I'll be in days that follow,*
> *I'll remember happy days at Happy Hollow.*

**NOTE TO SELF:** Good things, unfortunately, end. But then you have good memories forever and ever!

# Humphrey's Top 10 Things to Pack for Camp

~•~•~•~•~•~•~•~•~•~•~•~•~•~•~

1. Earplugs—just in case somebody has a whistle
2. Stickers—because you never know when you'll need one or more
3. A good book, some cards or a game for a rainy day
4. A cage—for protection—but preferably a cage with a lock-that-doesn't-lock so you can get out
5. Lotion—for poison ivy (which I HOPE-HOPE-HOPE hamsters don't get)
6. An interest in learning new things, like horseback riding, swimming and canoeing
7. A good cook—like Maria—who is generous with treats
8. Rope for tying knots because it looks like fun
9. A spirit of adventure—you'll need it
10. A friendly attitude—you'll make new friends, which is what camp is all about!

Bonus item: bongo drums if your camp allows them